AF865793

Vacation Self

ALEXANDRA
ROMANOFF

831 STORIES

831 Stories

An imprint of Authors Equity
1123 Broadway, Suite 1008
New York, New York 10010

Copyright © 2026 by 831 Stories Inc.
All rights reserved.

Cover design by C47
Book design by Scribe Inc.

This is a work of fiction. Names, characters, places, and incidents either are products of the author's imagination or are used fictitiously.

Most Authors Equity books are available at a discount when purchased in quantity for sales promotions or corporate use. Special editions, which include personalized covers, excerpts, and corporate imprints, can be created when purchased in large quantities. For more information, please email info@authorsequity.com.

No part of this publication may be reproduced, distributed, or transmitted in any form or by any means, including photocopying, recording, other electronic or mechanical methods, or for the purpose of training artificial intelligence technologies or systems, without the prior written permission of the publisher, except in the case of noncommercial uses permitted by copyright law.

Library of Congress Control Number: 2026938958
Print ISBN 9798893311525
Ebook ISBN 9781668157930

Printed in the United States of America
First printing

www.831stories.com
www.authorsequity.com

Praise for *Vacation Self*

"No one writes sexy and smart like Romanoff—spinning a love story in a lush, woodsy setting full of crackling tension. This is a romance for grown-ups, one that offers redemption and tenderness for all those who are lost. I never wanted it to end."

—Maurene Goo, author of
One and Only and *Throwback*

"*Vacation Self* is a real joy, I devoured it in one delicious gulp. Hot, tender, and compulsively readable—this is the very best kind of escapism."

—Laura Wood, author of *Under Your Spell*

"Sexy, fresh, and oh-so-fun, *Vacation Self* bursts with energy and love. Romanoff packs its pages with irresistible characters and a delicious, intoxicating romance. The only thing it left me wanting was more, more, more."

—Jennifer Niven, #1 *New York Times*
bestselling author

"Sobriety and desire are sometimes a dangerous combination—but it can also be exhilarating. This is that story."

—A. J. Daulerio, founder of The Small Bow
and former editor of Gawker and Deadspin

SUNDAY

I

MAGGIE

I've lived in New York since I was eighteen, but there's still something about getting behind the wheel of a car that feels like freedom. It doesn't matter that I've spent more than half my life taking trains and buses and long walks across the city's grid: When I turn the keys and hear an engine roar, the part of me that will always be sixteen and bored in the Chicago suburbs comes alive. She blinks open her eyes. *Finally.*

Not that the engine of this rental—a Hyundai Elantra whose interior has been doused in air freshener so astringent it smells of mouthwash—is *roaring*, per se. It's more like gently grumbling along Route 100 North toward St. John's Cross, Vermont. I left the expanse of I-87 behind well over an hour ago, but I still haven't quite reached the small town where I'll be spending the next week. Which is a good thing. I probably need as much space between me and the city as possible if I'm going to be able to actually relax.

It was threatening rain when I left Manhattan this morning, and the clouds stayed heavy and dark the whole drive. But when I finally turn off the main road and onto the path that leads to the Cabins, weak rays of sunshine start to filter through the cloud cover. The light catches on the leaves of sugar maple and birch trees, which are glorious with mid-autumn color, as well as the still-somehow-bright green of the grass below. There's no scaffolding or high-rises in sight. Instead, a hawk soars through the sky, riding the currents of air under its wings, just drifting.

And below it, there they are: the Cabins. Or, well, the cabins themselves aren't quite visible, but the hotel's main building is. It's long and low-slung, fitted together from cedar stacked like real-life Lincoln Logs. Picture windows look out onto the expanse of perfectly manicured lawn in front. Behind the lobby building there's an idyllic lake, and on its banks are the structures that give this place its name. Though they're hardly as rustic as it suggests. The one I'll be staying in has a wood-burning stove . . . as well as a several-thousand-dollar espresso machine.

I pull into the circular driveway and turn off the car. I made the drive straight through, stopping only to buy gas-station coffee and to pee, and it feels strange to be still again. I spend a long moment adjusting before cracking the door open and unfolding into the crisp October air.

I raise my hands to the sky, giving a full-body stretch. I'm pretty short—5′2″—but five hours in a car are kind to no one. Especially those of us who turned forty earlier this year. I take in a deep lungful of air, and it smells like damp earth, green things. There's a touch of char, probably one of those stoves at work in a distant cabin. I wonder if I can catch a glimpse of lightning coming over the hill. It is supposed to storm at some point, and I'm pleased that I made it before the sky inevitably breaks open.

I'm interrupted by the sound of a door opening behind me. I turn around to see a bellhop looking sheepish, like he isn't certain whether it's better customer service to approach immediately or step back and let me finish having my moment. "Hi, ma'am," he says. "Can I help you with your bags?"

His *ma'am* sends a wave of discomfort through me, even though I'm sure saying it is just as much a part of this guy's job as wearing a neat navy polo, one with the Cabins' subtle logo stitched over his heart. But I also don't feel like I've really earned his *ma'am* just yet.

"Just taking it all in for now," I reply. "But thank you."

He nods and disappears back inside. I inhale one deep breath, and then another. My inability to get through a simple interaction with a bellhop without having a mild existential crisis is exactly why I need this vacation. Lately everything—even the supposedly nice things in my life—has felt tense and tiring. When I go to the flower market in the morning for work, the buckets of peonies and dahlias read as blank as squares on a spreadsheet. Even making dinner, something I usually enjoy, has turned into a chore, one more thing to get through. I can't tell if I just need a break from my routine or a new routine entirely—which would raise bigger concerns, given I already did a complete career 180 just five years ago. Hence the decision to spend a small fortune on a last-ditch attempt to get out of this funk and just, like, try to enjoy my life again.

I grab my bags and approach the hotel lobby doors,

which appear heavy but glide open with barely a touch. The requisite deer antlers hang over the front desk, but they've been strung with crystals to resemble something like a backcountry chandelier. I recognize Hayal Pozanti's dreamy abstract paintings covering the walls. The far corner of the room is taken up by a little bar-restaurant situation; according to the hotel literature, it serves drinks at night and breakfast every morning.

There's a woman behind the bar, carefully washing glasses. She's Asian and looks like she's probably in her early twenties. She has a distinct '90s Jenny Shimizu vibe, and I wonder if she's old enough to get that reference. Then my gaze lands—and sticks—on the man sitting across from her.

He's leaning, elbows atop the bar, so that I see him in perfect profile as he's laughing at something Young Jenny said. His head is thrown back, and his long, tan throat is on display. His smile is candid, revealing every crease and wrinkle: the crow's feet crinkling at the corners of his eyes and the smile lines grooved into his cheeks. It's the face of someone who's not pretending to be a day younger than he is, and a warm wave of desire rushes over me, something comforting and uncomplicated. It's almost as if I recognize him, even though I'm certain that we've never met before.

I've spent most of my life in New York surrounded by its wealthiest inhabitants, and I'm all too accustomed to how they smooth out their edges, make themselves look years younger with just a few vials of Botox, the exact right dose of filler. It's perfection, but it's also plastic. This man looks *alive*.

Time speeds back up as he recovers from that fit of laughter, and his gaze drifts across the room, suddenly meeting mine. His eyes are the deepest oceanic blue I've ever seen. His hair is a dark mess of cropped curls with salt threading through the pepper. As he realizes I've been watching, his mouth quirks up again into a teasing smirk.

I feel myself flushing up to the roots of my hair, and I'm pretty sure he can see that too. I'm so pale that everyone can always see when I blush. I spin around as fast as I can, and thank god, there's a navy-polo-clad employee striding up to the front desk, ready to check me in.

As I go through the formalities, I'm still thinking about the man: his smile, his eyes. If I were sixteen—my boldest, most reckless self—I would already be over there, sliding onto a neighboring barstool and ordering something with a cherry in it. At thirty, I might have completely ignored him, too busy climbing the corporate ladder to meet men who weren't clinging on to the same rungs.

Now at forty, I can't quite bring myself to go over and talk to him. He's so handsome that there's no way he's single, and anyway, I'm kicking off a vacation that's supposed to be all about me. This is not the time for random, albeit sexy, distractions.

But I have to admit that the clutch of longing I felt in my chest while watching him is the first real *want* I've experienced in ages. Something organic. An undeniable reminder that my body can want things other than work and sleep and Thai takeout. And I have to admit: There's something about this that feels like a good sign.

II

JAKE

My ass is slowly going numb. I shift in my seat, trying to rearrange my legs, but there's not really anywhere for them to go. On my right, a stack of boxes—probably new uniform polos by the looks of them—crowds up against my side. On my left, a push broom and a mop lean against the wall.

But Gemma is sniffling, rubbing the heels of her hands against her eyes as she tries to keep herself from full-on sobs, so I won't be going anywhere anytime soon.

Now my hamstrings are starting to tingle, so I have to try to sneak one foot past the mop's handle, toward the far wall. But the work boots I'm wearing are clunky, and before I know what's happening, my toe nudges the mop out of place, dislodging the broom, which clatters onto yet another messy stack of boxes and sends two careening off the top of their pile. They land with a heavy thud.

"Jesus *Christ*!" Gemma yelps, leaping to her feet. She manages to catch a third box, cradling it in her arms and closing her eyes as she takes a deep breath.

"Fuck, I'm sorry." I can finally stand upright and take

the carton from her, putting it back where it belongs and sliding the mop and broom into place. When I pick up the box that fell on the floor, its contents shift around in a way that sounds distinctly . . . broken.

"Ah, sorry," I repeat.

"It's all right." Gemma shrugs. "Probably a sign I've kept you trapped in here too long anyway."

"Gem, come on. It's fine."

Gemma gives me a familiar look. "It's not. And listen, Jake, it's not your fault you weren't built to fit in these things." She reaches up and pokes each of my shoulders, made broader by the workouts that help keep me sober. Even if I don't do anything especially useful with the muscle I've packed on.

"I want to be here for you," I insist, poking her back.

"You *are* being here for me," she says. "This isn't even really, like . . . you know. Serious. I'm venting, or whatever. It's just the postbreakup blues."

That's part of the deal we made when we first started doing these impromptu two-person AA meetings: that we could always come to each other for sanity checks, for ugly confessions, or to curb an oncoming emotional outburst. It's one of the best deals I've ever made, sobriety-wise, but sometimes I wish that fewer of these meetups took place in the Cabins' various supply closets.

Honestly, I like that Gemma comes to me with just as many low-grade problems as more pressing ones; she's probably the only person in the world who thinks of me as a confidant. But it's too much to dig into when her shift starts so soon. "She wasn't good enough for you anyway," I say instead of something more helpful.

Gemma grins and shakes her head at me. "You would say that."

All I can do is smile and shake my head in return. Gem and I met a few years ago; she never knew me in my wild twenties, when I more than earned the nickname "Jackass Jake," or even before that, when I was a boy-band hellion who thought it was very mysterious to go by his last name: Ramsey. It's not just that she lets a forty-two-year-old bachelor with exactly zero successful relationships under his belt give her love-life advice. It's that she believes this version of me is the real one. I both relish her faith in me and live in fear of the day I could betray it.

"I should get back out there anyway." Gemma smooths a hand across her buzz cut. "I am on in five."

"You sure? I know you don't like letting Abe run things alone, but he can probably handle—"

Gemma dismisses the idea with a flick of her wrist. "He tried to make someone a French 75 with whiskey last night. He absolutely cannot be left unsupervised. Plus, it's good for me to be distracted. You know. From the wallowing."

I can't argue with her there. One of the reasons Gem and I get along so well is that we're both compulsively busy people. If we don't give our hands something productive to do, they will find something self-destructive to fill the void.

And also: Maybe that woman will still be out there. The one I saw earlier. After Kelsey and I broke up, I swore off dating for the foreseeable future, but looking isn't off-limits.

It's like Gemma can hear Kelsey's name cross my mind. Or she can read it on my face. "Are you gonna head home?" she asks, glancing over her shoulder as we make our way out into the lobby. "I do have to work, but we didn't even get to talk about how you've been doing since—"

Gem was understandably curious when I showed up in town a few weeks ago; I'm rarely here this late in the fall. At the time, I waved it off, told her that I'd been traveling too much and needed to take a break somewhere slow and quiet. But the tabloid headlines about Maya and Charlie's wedding haven't stopped—and neither have the accompanying reports about me: his former bandmate's most-recent breakup. Gem knows me well enough not to push, but apparently she's tired of waiting for me to be the one to bring it up.

"That's not a big deal." I close the supply closet door, trying to avoid eye contact. "And anyway, I really gotta—"

I'm so busy trying to avoid explaining myself that I'm not looking where I'm going, and suddenly my hands are pressed against something warm and soft.

Not something. Someone.

It happens just like it did from across the lobby, only this time, her face is much closer. Her espresso-dark eyes go wide, and her full mouth parts in surprise. She's had time to go back to her room and change, I notice. Her hair was pulled back from her face earlier, but it's down now, a cascade of soft chestnut. My hands have somehow landed at the bend of her waist, skimming the surface of her cashmere sweater, and I can feel all too precisely how at home my palms feel there.

For the second time in about five minutes, I hear myself repeat, "Oh, fuck, I'm sorry."

"It's fine," she says, taking a half-step back and breaking the accidental embrace. "Looks like we're heading to the same place."

We're not, actually. I was about to go home and heat up one of the meal delivery kit things that have been sustaining me ever since I arrived here two weeks ago. But instead of contradicting her, I follow her the last few feet toward the bar. She slides onto a stool, and I do the same, leaving one respectful seat between us. So she can ignore me if she wants.

Then I angle my body toward her anyway. Listen, I didn't make four separate trips to rehab because I was *good* at resisting temptation.

She doesn't seem to notice. Instead, she pulls a book out of her bag, places it in front of her, and picks up the menu to peruse.

"You want anything, Jake?" Gemma asks. She looks puzzled, and that's fair. Thirty seconds ago, I was in the middle of explaining that I couldn't possibly spend another second at the hotel. Now I'm settling in like I've got all the time in the world.

"Um. Yeah. Could I get—do you guys still have that lemon ginger tea from a few weeks ago?"

"Of course." She turns to the woman. "And do you need a minute, or—?"

"A glass of champagne," she says with a nod. "And probably food, too, but I don't know what yet."

"Well, I'm happy to give you recommendations if you want, but really, everything on the menu is good." Gemma moves to grab our glasses, already slipping into professional mode. I can see the way that it dissolves some of the strain that was gathering around her eyes during our conversation.

The woman scans the menu, her mouth curving into an anticipatory smile. And despite what I thought earlier about the harmlessness of looking, I have to turn away. This is not what I do here. This is not who I am here.

I first started coming out to the Cabins a couple of decades ago, in an attempt to dry out. It usually worked while I was on the hotel grounds, but it never once stuck after I left the quiet of St. John's Cross. Still, when I finally managed to get sober, one of the first things I did was buy a place just a few miles out of town.

It's been my retreat ever since, and I've always been careful not to sully it with hookups—certainly not with locals, because this town is way too small for that kind of thing, but not with hotel guests either. I want there to be one place in the world where I can at least pretend to be a stand-up guy.

Gemma busies herself pouring; the woman opens her book. I really should leave, but I was dumb enough to sit down and order something, so I can't cut out without looking even weirder. I check my phone, but the only message is from Devin, in the Mischief group chat: a picture of his teenage daughter playing at a local open mic night. I do a double-tap to heart it. I've yet to want kids of my own, but it's impossible to not adore a kid like Opal.

Gemma returns with my mug and the woman's flute. "I'm Gemma, by the way, and I'm here for anything else you need."

"Nice to meet you, Gemma," the woman replies. "I'm Maggie."

"Well, welcome to the Cabins, Maggie." Gemma glances at the book. "Oh! Is that the new Shera Benoit?"

Maggie nods. "I love her stuff. When I saw that this was coming out the week of my vacation, it felt like fate."

"Jake is the person who recommended her to me, actually." Gemma nods in my direction.

"Oh, really?" All of a sudden, Maggie's focus—actually, Maggie's entire body—has shifted my way. It feels like there's nowhere safe to put my gaze. I settle on her eyes.

I have to clear my throat, like I haven't spoken for hours. "I met her at a party," I say. "Shera. She made me laugh." I don't add that it was quite a feat, given the circumstances. I had agreed to do a favor for a friend and ended up at a "salon" hosted by one of the most boring people on the planet: some tech dude, Henry Jacobson, the kind of man who thought being wealthy meant he could buy himself a personality and, failing that, rent ours for the evening. If I hadn't been seated next to Shera, I probably would have faked my own death before the second course arrived.

Maggie grins. "She seems extremely cool."

"She was." I don't know if I've ever laughed as hard as I did watching Shera imitate our host trying to brag about his NFT art collection. Those terrible cartoon apes. "Her boyfriend too. I don't know if you've listened to his music—Max King?"

The name is just leaving my mouth as I feel the slap of a too-friendly hand on my back. "Are you bragging about your rockstar friends again, Ramsey?" a man's voice asks. Of course. Eric. The Cabins' concierge loves to name-drop, even when he's just dropping your own name back to you.

I watch helplessly as Maggie wordlessly puts two and two together: *Jake* and *Ramsey* and *met Shera Benoit and Max King at a dinner party*. We're about the same age; she could have any number of horrible headlines to pull from. Is she flashing back to the time I fell on stage during a Mischief concert—wasted, naturally—and broke my nose? Did she read the sanctimonious interview I gave to *People* magazine a few months out of my first rehab stint, and did she follow it when I very publicly relapsed the day after it was published? *People* added an update at the top of the article.

Suddenly, all the buoyancy I had felt when we first locked eyes falls flat. I can't stomach hearing her personal highlight reel of famous former boy-bander Jake Ramsey's mistakes—not when I review them myself so often. So I return Eric's bro hug a little too heartily. "You know me," I say. "But I was just heading home, actually. Gem, can you put this on my tab? Nice to meet you, Maggie."

It's stupid, repeating her name, even saying goodbye, like it matters at this point. At least I manage not to make eye contact with her again before I flee.

MONDAY

III

MAGGIE

I wake up feeling . . . lost. I'm not allowing myself to check work emails. Yesterday, I set an out-of-office, deleted the app from my phone, and told my assistant to text if there was a floral emergency. I don't have any client meetings or appointments, and that means I also don't have to try to cram eating and working out and socializing around them. There's literally nothing to structure my day. Except for, well, whatever I want to do.

I'm starting to realize that I actually don't know what that is.

As I brush my teeth, I leave my phone in the bedroom, and instead of cranking the volume of *The Daily* and panicking about the news, I focus on the taste of spearmint and the light moving in the fir trees outside the bathroom window. My own reflection is faint in the glass, mostly just shapes and shadows. *There I am*, I think, and then immediately after: *What does that even mean?*

One thing I know I want is some coffee, and I make myself a latte with the cabin's gleaming La Marzocco espresso machine and take it out onto my front porch. My hair is sleep-wild, and I'm braless, but the cabins are positioned for maximum privacy. And who am I trying to impress anyway?

Jake Ramsey, elbows on the bar, flashes through my mind. But he is *a literal celebrity*, not some shockingly handsome local. I did a little shame-googling after I got back to my cabin last night and discovered that not only has his most-recent ex been on the cover of *Sports Illustrated*'s Swimsuit Issue, but she's also at least fifteen years younger than both me and Jake. Whatever little spark I thought I felt when we met yesterday—and however good it felt to end up accidentally pressed against him, even if ever so briefly—that's just the charm and charisma and good looks of a seasoned entertainer working their magic.

That knowledge didn't stop me from examining pictures of Jake and Kelsey Turcotte for an embarrassingly long time, from zooming in on images from about a month ago: the two of them leaving the Brooklyn restaurant where Jake's old bandmate Charlie had just married his girlfriend, Maya McPherson. Jake and Kelsey looked serious and somber, holding hands but not smiling, though perhaps they were annoyed to be caught in the paparazzi's flash. Another google confirms that Charlie and Maya did everything they could to keep the wedding private, but someone had leaked the details to the press.

Next came an *Us Weekly* article about Jake and Kelsey's breakup, liberally peppered with quotes that seemed like they had come straight from the mouth of a seasoned publicist: reassurances that Kelsey was "so busy" and "really wanted to have more fun before settling down." The rep was likely Kelsey's, and the article managed to imply without ever quite outright saying so that Jake's sobriety was harshing his girlfriend's carefree twentysomething mellow.

Only then did I finally put my phone down and force myself to get ready for bed. But just because I wasn't still looking at photos of Jake didn't mean I wasn't still thinking about him. What I really couldn't shake, even as I started to nod off, was the look on his face when he realized I had figured out who he was. How quickly he shut down, like he was certain that whatever I'd realized couldn't be good. I can't imagine everyone in the world knowing every last, terrible detail of the worst things I've ever done. How I would feel if Jake could just conjure up quotes from the last guy who'd said I worked too much to be "girlfriend material" from a cursory internet search.

Old habits die hard, and I thoughtlessly bring my phone out to the porch. It pulls me out of my thoughts as it lights up with a text.

Angela: *Where are my pictures???*

I snap the almost-too-idyllic scene in front of me: the morning light reflected soft and pale across the lake, surrounded by the dense near-black of a stand of conifers.

Caught you, is her response. *Why are you looking at your phone at 8 a.m.?*

I roll my eyes. It would be nice, in theory, to have a best friend who wasn't a complete maniac. But then how could she even understand me?

I wasn't until you texted. I don't even know how many emails I have right now.

Wow, look at you. What are your plans for the day?

I tap my fingers against the phone's glass. My no-plan plan does have a loophole: The Cabins offers ample programming to help neurotic city-dwellers cosplay at relaxing. I pull up the "Activities" page on their website and am hit with an array of appropriately Zen-sounding options: yoga, Pilates, aromatherapy workshops, watercolor classes, guided hikes. The first yoga class starts in half an hour, held in the hotel's de facto activity center, which, of course, is called the Barn. I doubt it at all resembles anything on an actual working farm, but I'm willing to go find out. Tire myself out a bit. Kill time between now and lunch.

It's definitely sad that I'm already looking for ways to "kill time" on the first day of my vacation, but it's not like I know what else to do.

I text Angela back, *A little yoga. Then just . . . seeing what happens from there.*

That's my Maggie, she writes back. *She's just been promoted to the CEO of relaxing.*

When I walk into the yoga studio, there's a teacher sitting at the front of the room, pulling her long, glossy hair into a ponytail as she chats with one of the students. A few people have already set up their mats, and I spread one out in the back row. I fit in a run whenever I can, but I haven't done any real stretching in years. Without a phone in hand, I'm not really sure what to do with myself, so I sit down and pull my legs into a familiar butterfly position and try to experience the sensation of the tug across my hips.

There's an older woman sitting in front of me who moves with the ease of someone who practices self-care like it's a religion. She's already in lotus posture, and I watch as she twists her spine so that she's nearly facing the back of the room. Her face is so familiar that I smile without quite meaning to. But she doesn't smile back, and after a second, I realize why.

I've been to this woman's house a hundred times, but we've never actually met. In fact, on any other day, us being in the same room would be an expensive mistake on my part. Barbara Randolph is the matriarch of the Randolph family: daughter of late New York Senator Ian Randolph, and mother to socialite Kit Randolph. And I am Barbara Randolph's florist.

Her weekly deliveries are a gig that came to me by way of an industry friend who warned me that it would be lucrative, but weird—a crash course in the lives of the *ultra*rich. I communicate regularly with Barbara's household staff about events she has coming up or guests who might be visiting. I get periodic updates on her tastes and moods and whims. I could rattle off her approved colors and off-limits flowers. But for everything I know about Barbara Randolph, she has never spoken directly to me, and I slip in and out of her

Park Avenue home through a side entrance she wouldn't dream of using. Her arrangements are the steady, heartless work that I came here to escape.

I fold forward, despite my body's protesting. How did I not see this coming? The Cabins is a famously beloved destination of New York's elite. I start chastising myself. I should have found somewhere farther away, or quieter, or less well known. I'm trying to get a break from my life, and I'm already being reminded of what's soul-crushing about it. The gears in my head start their grinding: *What if I can't manage to relax while I'm here? What if I can never truly relax again? Have I screwed up my life so irreparably that—*

The teacher's announcement to come into cat-cow prevents me from entering a full-on spiral. After that, the class is mercifully fast paced, designed to keep everyone's arms and abs toned, even on vacation. I lose myself in the movement as best I can.

By the time we're done, I feel physically better, but my stubborn brain is eager to jump right back to it. Because despite my creative woes, money's been good this year—good enough for me to splurge on this stay—but also, it's impossible to know what the future holds. Will I have a good holiday season? Will I be able to give my assistant, Viola, the hours they want, and will they leave if I can't? What if this job becomes a spiritual *and* financial disaster?

These thoughts rush through my mind, and I'm barely able to take in the scenery around me on my walk back to the cabin. When I quit my day job in finance to be a florist full time, it felt like a jailbreak: an opportunity to ditch Bloomberg Terminal and Excel and live in a world populated entirely by creative people and plants. But the truth of running a small business is that the spreadsheets follow you wherever you go. And the screens do too.

My original plan had been to stay on the Cabins' grounds the whole time I'm here, but the hotel feels suffocating, and I decide to take myself to a nearby farm that makes fresh sandwiches daily with bread, cheese, and preserves made on-site. I'd saved it on my map when I planned the trip as an "in case of an emergency" excursion, and I try to give myself grace for using my escape hatch so early. *This is what you want right now*, I tell myself. It's only a few miles away, so I borrow one of the Cabins' many bikes and pedal my way down the long driveway and out onto the road.

It's Vermont in mid-October, and the air is chilly as it whips at my cheeks and through my hair. But soon my heart is pumping in time with my legs. I breathe deep and smell pine and water and maybe even the first hint of winter. Despite the morning's worries, for the first time in I don't know how long, biking through St. John's Cross, I feel something approaching a sense of calm.

IV

MAGGIE

Perry Hill Farm's barn couldn't be more different from the one where I did sun salutations this morning. Here there's no sprung wooden floor, just dirt and some leftover hay rustling softly underfoot. The only lighting comes through windows in the lofted ceiling, so it's dim and quiet, almost churchlike. A refrigerator hums while it works. A few folding tables are laid with dusty root vegetables, jarred jams, and exactly two remaining wax paper–wrapped sandwiches.

I grab one of the sandwiches and slip a twenty into the box marked simply, PAY WHAT YOU OWE. Of course there's no way to make change, and that makes me smile.

The combination of morning yoga and the brisk bike ride has left me starving, and since there's no signage or menu, I'm now wildly curious what today's sandwich contains. When I peel back a corner of the paper, the fresh-baked scent of yeast and flour greets me. I bite into it and taste the sweetness of roasted beets, the tang of goat cheese, a peppery hit of arugula, all blasted with an herby vinaigrette. It's like one last little breath of summer.

I'm still chewing when I hear the sound of footsteps approaching. I glance up toward the door to see Jake Ramsey walking through.

He's wearing a cream wool sweater and a navy beanie. There's something about the shape of his body—the length of his legs, the way his arms confidently swing as he walks—that makes my chest go tight. I'm standing, but he's so tall that I have to tilt my head further to meet his gaze.

I swallow as fast as I can, and his eyes go wide as he recognizes me. "Oh," he says. And then, "I mean, uh, hello again."

"Hello again." I know I'm blushing, but there's nothing to do about it.

"How did you—did Gemma recommend this place to you?"

"No. Eater. They did a profile of the chef at the Cabins, and he mentioned it."

"Someone's gotta tell Tarik to stop blowing up our spots." Jake shakes his head and wags his brows.

"Well, I did save you the last sandwich." I gesture to the table.

A smile lights up his face exactly the way it did yesterday across the lobby, and I feel the same warmth flooding my chest. "Thank god. Although if I had missed it, it would have been my fault. I meant to come earlier. I just got caught up working on a project, and all of a sudden I looked up and it was . . ." He scans the room for a clock. "Whatever time it is now."

When he left last night, it seemed like he wanted his

privacy. I don't want to bother him. But I can't help myself. "What are you working on?"

"Just trying to build a bookcase. Right now I'm prepping the wood, which requires a lot of sanding. It's kind of meditative. Maybe too meditative, clearly, since I lost track of time."

"Ah, so you're the kind of guy who does chores at his vacation house."

Jake tugs off his hat and ruffles a hand through his hair. It looks darker, and he looks younger, in the low light. "It's not really a vacation house. And they're not chores. I've been trying to learn carpentry forever. So whenever I'm out here . . ." he trails off.

I regret the tease. I don't want him to feel like I'm trying to call him out. "Oh, I mean, I'm hardly one to talk. This is my first vacation in half a decade, and I didn't make it one full day before I had to give myself a field trip."

Jake laughs. It's a good laugh, throaty and conspiratorial. I feel for a second like we're getting away with something. Like we're in cahoots.

But then reality intrudes. Jake is still looking at me, and I become very conscious that my hair is still windblown from the ride over. I'm wearing leggings that I actually worked out in and a chore coat and sneakers that are more practical than fashionable. Basically, I look absolutely nothing like a twenty-six-year-old *Sports Illustrated* model.

But he doesn't look away.

"Were you planning on eating here?" he asks, after a moment.

"I just wanted to try it before I headed back. Give myself something to look forward to."

Jake nods. "You're impatient."

"I'm hungry."

The silence that follows feels too loaded for two people talking about sandwiches in a barn that also sells chicken feed.

Jake clears his throat. "Well," he says. "They have a picnic table here. So you don't have to bike all the way back, if you don't want."

I don't decide, exactly. My mouth just opens, and I hear myself speak: "Lead the way."

We step out of the barn and into the early afternoon sunlight. The rain held for a surprisingly long time last night, the storm only really breaking as I was going to bed. Now the day is crystalline, the sky so clear and blue that it almost hurts to look at. Jake guides me along a path dotted with milkweeds that skirts the edge of an empty field. It looks like it's been put to bed for the season: Whatever cover crop they'd planted has been mowed down and mulched over. The muted quiet from the barn is replaced by the sound of our feet crunching across browned grass.

"I'm lucky I found a local to show me the way," I say. "Or do you count as a local, if you also live in the city?"

Immediately I realize that I've given myself away—a real stranger wouldn't know about Jake's Tribeca apartment. But if he realizes that and is put off, he doesn't let on. "I could spend the rest of my life here and I wouldn't be a local," he says. "You know the thing people say, about the kittens?"

"The kittens?" I repeat.

"'Just because a cat has kittens in the oven doesn't make 'em biscuits,'" he recites solemnly. "Like, even if you're born here, they don't necessarily consider you one of them. Takes generations. And anyway, yeah, I'm a summers-only guy. The worst kind of visitor, really."

I shake my head. "Where I come from, it's all very Olive Garden. 'When you're here, you're family,' you know?"

Jake laughs. "Where are you from?" he asks.

"Chicago suburbs."

He glances at me sideways. "A Midwestern girl."

I shrug. "I guess."

"You guess?"

"It's just that I've lived in New York since I was eighteen. Sure, I have Midwestern roots, but what does that even count for, at this point?"

Jake pauses to look at me. We're deeper onto the property, and the grass around us is nearly knee-high. "I don't know," he says. "What *does* it count for?"

The question catches me off guard. By this point in my life, I've had a lot of time to try on identities, aesthetics, and lives. I've been an ambitious suburban teenager determined to get to the big city; I've been a big-city girl hell-bent on VP-track success. Now I'm a grown woman with her own business who's meant to be in charge of her own destiny. I always imagined that, at this point in my life, I'd know exactly who I was, what I wanted, and where I was going, but that's hardly my reality.

I can't bring myself to share any of that with this man I've just met. "I say soda instead of pop now," I tell him.

Jake laughs as he graciously allows me to dodge his question. "And what are you on vacation from, exactly?"

"I'm a florist. Which I know probably doesn't sound very stressful, but the way I do it, it is."

"Which is?"

"Full throttle."

That earns me another laugh. "Full-throttle florist," he repeats. "You sound like an action hero. Armed with pruning shears or something."

"I mean, not—the full throttle is . . . it's not the flowers that are stressful. It's mostly just running a small business. I do the arranging, and the deliveries, and also the customer service, and a lot of the administrative work. And in the midst of paying the bills and finding a new supplier for vases, I should somehow make space for creative fulfillment too."

We've arrived at a wooden, weather-beaten picnic table tucked under the beech trees that line the property. I take a seat, and Jake joins opposite me. "But the truth is that I would probably find a way to make any job hard on myself. That's certainly been my track record so far, anyway."

He nods thoughtfully, as if he's adding this to a store of information about me. Putting me together like a puzzle. "So that's why no vacations for a decade."

I unwrap my sandwich, take a bite, and swallow before answering. "Yeah. I was working in finance for a long time, and then I left to let myself breathe and try something new.

But once I started my business—Margaret, it's called, like my full name—" *Yeah, Maggie, he probably figured that out* "—that became crazy too. So I promised my friends—and myself—that I would lean all the way into this break. I'm here until Saturday, so this is my week of just doing whatever the fuck I want at all times."

Jake's eyes skate across my face, and a smile curves at the corners of his mouth. "I like the sound of that," he says. He takes a bite, and his words rumble through me, a low vibration against my skin.

I'm just imagining it, I assure myself, even though we're still making eye contact. The feeling that he's interested in what I want as anything other than casual conversation fodder.

"What's that going to look like?" he asks.

"I mean, so far it looks like nothing. Like not setting my alarm, and not checking my email. Like not having a plan for the rest of the day."

Against my will, my mind flashes to the vibrator I bought just before I left the city. I figured if I was really going to try to get back in touch with myself, that had to include sex too. So far, I'm describing this week to Jake like it's totally passive: putting down my everyday worries and vegging out. But the truth is that I'm also trying to actively want.

I watch his throat as he swallows a bite and rest my eyes on the collar of his fisherman knit instead. Even just thinking about sex in front of this man feels dangerous, like he'll be able to read the desire written all over my face if

I'm not careful. I grasp for a change of subject. "How did you get into carpentry?"

"I—I have a lot of hobbies," he stammers briefly. "When I got sober, I needed something to replace the drinking. Bookcase building is one of my somethings."

Last night, when that guy said his full name at the bar, Jake's face shut down; all the friendliness I had seen vanished so fast it was as if it had never been there at all. And now he just looks . . . cautious, I think. As if he wants to assess my reaction to the word *sober* and navigate accordingly. As if he cares how I feel about it.

"My best friend got sober right before I met her," I tell him. "Her something was embroidery. Kept her hands busy. The first time we hung out, she insisted on monogramming the shirt I was wearing."

Angela and I first met at a dinner for female entrepreneurs when I was in the early stages of launching Margaret, after doing bouquets at friends' requests for years. At that point, Angela's record store was a PowerPoint presentation and a dream. Before meeting her, I had never thought of myself as a "girl's girl"; I was too busy looking out for how other women might undermine me, which had served me well enough in banking, where there were only a few seats for us. "I'm not here to make friends," I might have even said, and meant it.

But Angela's openness disarmed me. We ended up at the same table, and when a server came by to offer her a drink, Angela held up a hand. "I'm six months sober." She must have seen how unnerved I was by her openness, because after the server walked away, she shrugged, grinning. "I figure the best way to keep myself honest is to *be* honest," she said.

At that point, I was not yet six months out of the finance world, where we all worked until the sun came up and repeatedly lied about "loving the grind." I had seen plenty of alcoholics try everything to cover up their sobriety in order to keep getting invited to drinks with the bosses; I had seen even more people refuse to admit they had a drinking problem for the same reason. Angela was suddenly the bravest person I'd ever met. I knew I would be stupid not to get to know her better.

Jake and I spend a few minutes eating quietly. Birds chirp in the trees; I listen to the sound of the wind moving over grass and through fire-orange sugar maple leaves. Without quite meaning to, I take in a full breath and let out a long sigh.

"What's going on over there?" Jake asks.

"Nothing," I say. "But nothing in a good way. I was just wondering when the last time I ate a meal like this was. No computer, no book, just . . . sitting here."

"St. John's Cross is good for that."

I almost instinctively ask a follow-up about his life in New York: about the wedding and the breakup. But I can't ask about that because I shouldn't *know* any of it. Though it feels stranger, at this point, not acknowledging the elephant in the room. I pause, trying to figure out how to phrase what I'm going to say next.

"I have to admit something," I start. "Last night, I didn't recognize you at first. But when that guy said your name—"

"Yeah," he says. "I saw."

"I'm sorry."

"What are you sorry for? Paying attention to pop culture in the late '90s? We were inescapable. Especially if you were a teenage girl at the time." His grin is sly, inviting, and I understand viscerally that if I had somehow met him back then, I would have been completely powerless against his charm. Not that I'm doing such a good job at resisting it now. And he's barely trying.

Jake seems to realize he could be mistaken for flirting, and he drops the grin as quickly as he'd flashed it. "Anyway. I take it you weren't a fan."

"I wasn't *not* a fan. I was just . . . interested in other things." That's one way of putting it. I had a bad case of *not like other girls* back then—thus my lack of female friendships. At the time, I would have strenuously denied the truth, which is that I enjoyed the shit out of Mischief's songs when I heard them on the radio or piped through the speakers in a drugstore. I was in such denial I couldn't even tell you who I found the cutest. I couldn't bring myself to look.

I guess now I know.

"Fair enough," Jake says.

"Anyway. It just felt weird not to say it." I look down at my lunch and realize how little of it is left. How soon it won't make sense for us to sit here talking like this.

He nods. "I appreciate it, actually. As weird as it is to talk about, it's actually weirder to talk around."

I take the final bite of my sandwich. "I feel like I owe you something," I say. "Like you should be able to ask me a nosy question about my life."

It's a half-joking offer, and maybe he can tell, but Jake's expression doesn't show it. "Did you google me?" he asks.

I nod, shamefaced.

"OK, then you probably know I just went through a breakup, so can we make it even here? When was your last one?"

He can't be fishing to find out if I have a boyfriend.

I fold up the wax paper in front of me. "Two years ago. We'd been together for almost a year. I was—" I almost say *in my late thirties*, but that's a cop-out. *Be honest, Maggie*, I think. It's not like he hasn't at least guessed the neighborhood of my age already. "Thirty-eight," I continue. "And people started asking if we were thinking about getting married. And the answer was . . . no. Not on my end, anyway. And after enough people had asked me that, and I had said no enough times, I realized that it wasn't just that I didn't want to marry him right then. I didn't really see any kind of future with him at all."

Jake chuffs out a laugh. "I don't think anyone's ever asked me if I was going to get married."

I've already pressed my luck as much as I feel like I can. I don't ask about the end of his relationship with not-yet-thirty-year-old Kelsey or what might have happened between them at Maya McPherson and Charlie Blake's wedding.

"That's because they don't know about the carpentry," I say. "Who wouldn't want to marry a man who knows what to do with his hands?"

I was aiming for a light, jokey tone, but as soon as the

words leave my lips, Jake's eyebrows shoot straight up. I feel my cheeks go crimson. Blushing always sounds cute in theory, but on my face, it's an immediate tell of all my feelings. My blood vessels are a fucking hazard.

"Anyway, I should probably let you get back to it," I say hurriedly. "The carpentry. And all."

Jake stands. "I do need to go start staining if I'm going to be able to actually finish this thing before I leave."

The two of us start walking back toward the barn, side by side. It's the time of year when the days are getting shorter and shorter, and although it's early, the sun already feels like it's sliding down through the western sky. I concentrate on making sure that our hands don't brush by accident.

"How long are you in town for?" I ask. "Since you're normally a summer guy."

"I have another three weeks, max. Then I'm heading to Berlin."

"Is that vacation? Or is this vacation?"

Jake purses his lips. "I mean, my whole life is kind of a vacation."

I laugh. "Vacation with chores."

"I told you, they're not—" he narrows his eyes playfully at me. "You're teasing me."

"I would never."

"I'm sure." He shakes his head, mock disappointed in me. "It's a good question though. Is this vacation . . . I'm gonna think about that."

"Well, I'm going to think about what you said earlier.

The question of what all my past lives add up to at this point."

As we stand in the parking lot facing each other, I realize what I've just admitted: that I'll be thinking about him.

And that he said he'll be thinking about me too.

Jake is the one to break the silence. "I hope you enjoy the rest of your trip. Get all your rest, do a lot of whatever you want to do."

I smile up at him, and he smiles back. The idea of not seeing him again—this small glimpse of him being all I get—slices through me like a paper cut: It's swift, but searing. It's enough to push the next sentence out of my mouth before I can really think it fully through, the words tumbling over one another in a rush. "If I wanted to see the best parts of this place while I'm here, what should I do?"

Jake contemplates this. He reaches his arms to the sky, stretching, and I cannot help looking to see if his sweater will pull up and give me a glimpse of his stomach or the ridge of his hip. But it's oversize enough that, even on a man this tall, it keeps him covered.

"I mean, the Cabins has everything you could want, pretty much," he says after a minute. "That's why you stay there, right?"

"No. Totally." I don't even know what I'm expecting him to say. I'm well aware that the only reason to go to St. John's Cross, Vermont, is to visit the Cabins.

Jake reaches across his body, adjusting his sleeve. "There's a hiking trail near my house," he says. "It just goes to a little pond. Probably three miles out and back. That's where I go when I need to think. But the quiet is like nothing else I've ever heard."

"What's the name of the trail?"

"Moon Lake. The only thing is that there's not a proper trailhead, so there's no real parking. People in the neighborhood just walk over, or you can leave your car on the side of the road."

"That sounds perfect," I say. "I'll do that."

Jake nods. "You could also . . ." he starts. "Well, the beginning of the trail runs across the back of my property. So you could also park at my place, if you wanted. Say hi on your way in, or out."

His gaze finds mine and stays there. For a long moment, I'm lost again in the tumbling blue of his eyes. *This is intimate*, I think. This offer. In these short encounters I've had, Jake's been easy to talk to, but I get the sense that he guards his privacy fairly carefully. It feels like it means something, him suggesting this to a woman he barely knows.

The weight of that thought snaps me back to reality. I'm probably making this a way bigger deal than it really is. Maybe Jake does this all the time—meets random women wherever he flits into town. Picks them up because he can.

But Jake is fiddling with his sleeve again, his fingertips nervous against the cuff and the skin of his inner wrist. He doesn't seem flip, or careless. He seems . . . he seems like he's waiting to hear what I'm going to say.

"If I were to come by tomorrow?" I ask. "In the morning. Would that work?"

"Yes," he says. "Yes, absolutely."

V

JAKE

She's not actually going to come. I spend the rest of the afternoon repeating it like a mantra: *She's not actually going to come.*

I left Maggie with my phone number and a loose plan, and I pass the rest of the day urging myself to *be serious.* This is an adult woman who cannot realistically be interested in spending her precious vacation with some washed-up pop star who hasn't figured out how to sit still for twenty minutes at a time, let alone how to date a woman his own age.

But my brain is, as always, my own worst enemy. *The way she looked at you, though*—stop it. *It seemed like maybe she was feeling*—leave it, Jake. Leave it alone.

This cycle repeats over and over, and eventually I have to add an addendum for a bit of reprieve: *Even if she does come, it won't mean anything.*

If Maggie comes, it will be because she wants to get away from the Cabins, which can feel a little suffocating sometimes. At best, because she's interested in the trail. At worst—well, it wouldn't be the first time I've served as a spot on someone's vacation bingo card. *Fuck a celebrity*: check. I'm a priceless souvenir to take back to New York.

And as badly as I want to touch her—to fill my hands with her, to hear the sounds she makes in response—I already know that I can't do it that way. There's nothing worse than getting fucked like a trophy: a funny story someone will be able to tell and retell for the rest of their life, a piece of pop-culture trivia that happens to also have a dick.

Then again, she doesn't seem like the type. But it's hard to know.

I try and fail not to think about Maggie the full-throttle florist while I paint a coat of stain over the shelves of the bookcase. I try and fail not to think about her while I clean up my workspace. I try and fail not to let myself think about her in her shower, not to picture her joining me: water beading on the tops of her shoulders, on the fringe of her eyelashes, on the tips of her nipples. Her cheeks would be already flushed from the heat, and go even pinker when I—

She's not going to come.

As I finish getting dressed, hair still dripping, my phone lights up on the dresser. Whatever I've been trying to tell myself, my heart jackrabbits so fast that I almost go lightheaded. I have to pause and take a long, deep breath before I pick it up.

"Charlie Blake" flashes on the screen. It's accompanied by a picture of him at the band's annual holiday reunion, Chrismischief, a few years ago, sprawled on the couch at Devin's, wearing an ugly Christmas sweater Opal knitted for him. He looks as silly as he's ever looked, which really isn't very. Charlie's a serious bastard and always has been. It's one of the many ways we are nothing alike.

Charlie isn't the oldest member of Mischief—it's Chris, not that he'd ever admit it—but he was always the most responsible by a mile. He's picked up after me since we were teenagers, and at some point, I shifted from resenting him to being jealous of his ability to do so.

I answer the phone and put him on speaker. "What's up, Blake?"

"Hey, Rams. How are you doing?"

"Good," I reply, quickly. And then, because honesty really is supposed to be part of my sobriety practice, I revise. "I mean, you know. Fine."

"I heard you were up in Vermont." He says it casually, but I get the sense he has questions.

"Yeah, yeah, just wanted to make sure the place was ready for the winter." So much for honesty. "There were some issues with the roof last year, so I'm just getting it all checked out."

"Does that mean you're coming back to the city soon?"

I pull on my socks while I consider this question. I don't really have a return date in mind. When I got here, I figured I would cross that bridge when I came to it. When—*if*—I didn't feel such a pressing need to hole up and hide out, I would decide when to make a grand return to New York.

"Pretty soon," I say. It's avoidant, and I wait to see if Charlie will let me get away with it.

"Well, I actually called to ask you a favor. One of Maya's clients, Elena Perez, is eyeing a congressional run next year. And we're trying to put together a fundraiser for her."

"Oh, yeah. Just tell me who to make the check out to, man."

Charlie laughs. "We were actually hoping you might be game to say a few words. At the event."

Look, I can barely even talk to you right now, you can't possibly want me, I want to tell Charlie, but I'm struck silent. He keeps going. "She's done a lot of work trying to create addiction resources in her district. Moving money from the NYPD to counselors and rehab beds, that kind of thing. There's a constituent who got sober with help from the city, and the hope was you could kind of be in conversation with him. Just like, twenty or thirty minutes. He'd do most of the talking."

I open my mouth to reply and close it again.

"I understand if you don't want to," Charlie continues, his voice quieter, more gentle. "But I did want to ask you, Ramsey."

My name is such a funny thing. I started going by Ramsey in middle school. I was still waiting on my growth spurt, and I thought it sounded tougher than Jake. So that's what Charlie and Devin and Chris called me when we started hanging out, and that's what they were calling me when Mischief blew up a few years later. It became my public name: the thing that gets shouted at me when I'm walking down the street, what I might scrawl across a headshot or along a forearm when I used to be regularly asked for an autograph. I've watched thousands of different strangers look at me, confused, trying to will my name to the front of their brain. *Is that guy from that band? Mischief . . . right? And he was—Richard? Randolph? Rudolph?* When someone calls me Ramsey, it's a tell that they don't really know me, and never will.

Other than Charlie. When Charlie calls me Ramsey—or, more often, Rams—it sounds like home.

"When is it?" I ask.

"November. The week before Thanksgiving. So you've got some time to think about it. My's happy to talk to you about it too, if you want. She's here right—"

"No," I cut in. "Thank you, but I'm good for now."

Charlie's smart, but he's got a soft spot for my shit. It means he lets me get away with stuff every now and again. Maya's more perceptive, far too likely to ask some questions and get me saying all kinds of personal things I don't want to admit in the process of doing something as pedestrian as preparing opening remarks for some sort of fundraiser like this. That's basically how she and Charlie fell in love.

I was suspicious of her when we first met. All I knew was that she was a former fan who was currently clouded in scandal, and despite those red flags, Charlie was completely and utterly gone on her.

But the reality of Maya took the wind right out of my sails. The way she looked at him, the way she talked to me, both bored of my bullshit and somehow completely willing to put up with it. I'm not sure I knew what love—real, lasting, adult love—looked like up close until I started hanging out with the two of them.

And the thing is: Life was easier before that. When I didn't know what I was missing. That I was missing anything at all.

Thinking of my own romantic failings shakes something loose: a reminder that I actually can't do this event after all. That's the week I have plans to be in Berlin, helping an ex—Katia—set up an installation she's doing at Kunstraum Kreuzberg. I'm mostly bad at staying in touch with former girlfriends, but she and I didn't date for long, and we always made more sense as friends: two creative people who couldn't stay in one place for too long. Now I'm more like her ad hoc studio assistant: I'll always help put together her massive, industrial projects—wherever in the world they happen to be. She gets free labor; I get an excuse to leave.

When I tell Charlie that the timing won't work, he takes the news in stride. "Some other time, then," he says. Having gotten out of doing this thing I wasn't sure I wanted to do in the first place, I instantly feel bad. I owe Charlie a lot. It's not like he's asking for much or asks often. I really should come through for this kind of favor.

But he doesn't dwell. "One more thing, and then I'll let you go," he says. "I was just wondering if you'd talked to Kelsey at all? Since the breakup?"

I shake my head, even though I know he can't see me. I can never get a very good read on what Charlie thinks of my various age-inappropriate girlfriends, but he seemed to like Kelsey more than the others. "No," I say, then let the silence hang between us.

"OK." He waits again to see if I'll offer up anything else, but I don't take the bait. "I'm just wondering, did something happen, or . . ."

"What always happens," I say, which actually isn't totally

accurate. Usually I'm the one getting dumped, instead of being the person who has to say the dreaded *We need to talk*.

Which was horrible. After I did it, I felt like I should call up everyone who's ever had the guts to end it with me and thank them for being brave enough to save me that particular misery.

"It's just that you guys seemed pretty good at the wedding."

Did we? That's not the part of the wedding I remember. And really, that's why we broke up. Because even with her by my side, watching Charlie and Maya, I was still dreaming about something else. Something bigger. Something *more*. Something like—

"She's special. A good person. Really fucking funny," I say. And she is. She's just . . . young. And I have finally gotten to a place where I'm tired of pretending that I still am. Not only that; I don't really want to be. It's not Kelsey's fault that she hasn't had her Saturn return yet, but I'm more than a decade past mine. I was tired of explaining my jokes to her and of what people assumed when they saw us. Mostly that they were right to assume.

I try to move the conversation back to Charlie. "Speaking of the wedding, how was the honeymoon?"

"God. It was so good," he says warmly. "Maya didn't even bring her work phone. I wrote two new songs. I'll play them for you next time I see you."

I'm happy Charlie is happy, but my pickled little heart spasms at the idea of new music. It's not about the songs per se; I loved to perform, but I was never really an artist like that.

What pains me is the image of Charlie with Maya in their beautiful apartment. Sitting at the piano while she mixes them drinks. It's the life he deserves, and he should have it.

No, what pains me is that I want a version of that for myself.

For decades I've dated the shiniest, prettiest women I could find: girls whose sparkle I thought might counteract my darkness. But no matter how long we were together, I never felt settled. Never felt comfortable. Watching how Charlie and Maya lean on each other—I've understood, for the first time, why everyone harps on about finding a *partner*. Watching them at their wedding, I imagined for the first time what it would be like to have one.

Which also forced me to confront all the reasons I don't. How aimless my life is most of the time; how I'm busy but ultimately unproductive. How many years I've wasted on the worst, shallowest kinds of desires. How could I possibly meet the kind of woman I was imagining when I never stay in one place for more than a few months at a time? And why would that woman even want me, when I couldn't achieve any sort of emotional follow-through?

Ever since I first laid eyes on her, Maggie has felt like the universe pressing its fingers into my fresh bruises. Here is, at least at a glance, everything I've been asking for. A real opportunity to try.

And a real opportunity to fuck up.

But I've spent decades making my problems Charlie's problems, so I don't say any of that aloud. "I'll call you when I get back to the city and we'll catch up," I tell him instead.

TUESDAY

VI

MAGGIE

My second morning at the Cabins comes easier than the first. I brush my teeth and wash my face in the sunlit quiet, drink my coffee listening to birds in the firs. This place will hand-deliver breakfast, but I want to move. I want crisp air in my lungs.

So I head over to the main building. It's early enough that it's still quite cold, and the grass sparkles with ice-crystal dew. I tug my thick cardigan around me and pause on the path, tilting my face up to the sky for a few seconds, my exhalation unfurling as vapor. The sun is shining, and I soak it up. This is probably the most vitamin D I'll be getting for months.

As I decide between local yogurt and honey, a pear-custard pastry, and any preparation of farm-fresh eggs I could want, I notice a dark-haired man sitting at the bar, reading the newspaper. For a second, I fool myself into thinking it's Jake.

It doesn't even really look like him upon second glance. But I recognize my eagerness to see him again, and it embarrasses me. Especially after being in such a state about him last night that I called Angela to talk her through my lunch with him.

"Great, so you go to his place tomorrow, you hook up, and you call me after that. I love this plan," she said.

"You're skipping the most important part," I countered. "We don't even know if he wants that."

I could practically hear Angela rolling her eyes through the phone. "Of course he wants you."

"But also—"

"But nothing," she interrupted me smoothly. "*You* want *him*, right?"

There was no point in denying it. "Yeah."

"And what is this vacation supposed to be about, exactly?"

In another life, Angela is a vicious and successful lawyer. Her argument was undeniably sound. "Doing whatever I want," I answered, flopping back on the bed.

"There it is." Angela paused for a moment to celebrate her little victory. When she started talking again, her voice was more serious. "I mean it, Maggie. Forget all that bullshit about who he is and who he's fucked before you. You met a hot guy on vacation. He's nice to talk to and makes you feel good. I'm not saying you have to do anything *dramatic*, but why not pursue this *want* and see what happens, at the very least?"

It felt too silly to admit: I didn't want to feel stupid. Ever since I got here and first saw Jake's face, I've been living in a soap bubble made of hope and desire. I'd rather stay inside, with a shimmering film between me and reality, than find out what it feels like when it pops.

Angela took my silence as her cue to push a little harder. "You deserve this," she said, and I knew I wasn't going to get anywhere arguing *that* point, so I let the subject drop. At the end of the pep talk, I was still dubious. But I also realized I wouldn't have called Angela if I was looking for someone to talk me out of this feeling.

I want to spend as much time outside as possible, so I take my coffee and croissant out to the wooden chairs that border the lake. There's a small herb garden nearby; it fills my nose with the familiar smells of sage and rosemary.

It turns out to be the perfect spot for both breakfast-eating and people-watching. Servers deliver picnic basket breakfasts to guests, and groundskeepers roll by on golf carts, their rakes and leaf blowers strapped into the back seats. A guest in her twenties jogs by, not a single ounce of sweat staining her Lululemon set; an older couple in matching Patagonia moves at a more sedate pace. I wonder if I'll spot Barbara Randolph again, but she doesn't appear. I'm grateful.

I'm about halfway through my latte when a figure starts making its way down the path directly toward me. Gemma, the bartender. Jake's friend.

She's wearing the Cabins' uniform: dark pants and that navy polo, though its logo is covered by her oversize Carhartt jacket. Her pants are carelessly tucked into a pair of Blundstones. Even in clothes designed to make her blend in, she's beautiful and so deeply, obviously cool. I'm struck by a useless pang of jealousy: She looks like Jake's type. At least, more than I do.

She smiles politely at first—then, after she recognizes me, a little bit wider, realer. "Hey," she says. "Maggie, right?"

"And you're Gemma."

"I am." She pulls a long mesh bag out of one of her jacket pockets. "Harvesting some thyme to infuse into the simple syrup for tonight. Let me know if I'm in your way."

"Oh, no, please. Go right ahead."

There's a small red utility knife holstered at her waist; as I watch, Gemma unsheathes it and bends down to start clipping the herbs. Her movement is as familiar to me as breathing, and I have to shake the urge to offer to help. It reminds me so much of my own work, but not in the panic-inducing way that seeing Barbara at yoga did yesterday.

"How much of what you use at the bar do you grow on-site?" I ask.

"Oh, as much as we can." Her hands keep moving while she talks, the motion quick and practiced. "This patch is just for show, mostly—we have a much bigger garden with greenhouses and everything over there." She gestures vaguely to the other side of the lake. "It's one of the reasons I love working here. I'm sober, so a lot of the bar program is . . . not really my speed anymore. But I get to work with our Ag guys on what's in season and how to preserve and transform it. And that keeps it interesting and fun for me."

Ah. She's sober too. I wonder if that's how she and Jake got to be friends. Or whatever they are. "What's the thyme for?" I ask.

"The drink's called Thyme & Thyme Again." She raises a brow. "It's a pun," she deadpans. "I don't name the drinks, obviously."

"Even if you did, I wasn't going to judge you."

She shrugs. "You should. The name's awful." Her bag is now filled with thyme sprigs, and she stands. "What are you planning on doing between now and cocktail hour? Got any exciting plans?"

I feel an opportunity being handed to me. The universe is practically begging me to do a little recon on Jake. But I still hesitate. I look down at my phone, which I'm spinning anxiously between my fingertips, as if there might be something on my calendar. I pick up my coffee cup, but it's empty, down to the last dregs.

Gemma stands there, waiting for my answer.

"Actually," I say. "Jake—from the bar the other night—your friend?" She doesn't seem to flinch at my use of the word *friend*. "I went to Perry Hill Farm yesterday to get a sandwich, and we ran into each other?" It's not a question, but I hear my tone creep upward as if it could be. I force myself back into the declarative. "And he mentioned this hiking trail near his house. So I was thinking I might go check that out."

I brace for impact, waiting for Gemma to say that she'll probably be there when I stop by, so I should stop in and say hi. Or something like, "Oh, that particular spot is *quite* popular with a lot of female guests at the Cabins." Maybe she'll just shake her head, give me that silent girl-code nod: the implication that being alone with Jake isn't a good idea.

Instead, she just . . . looks a little harder at me. Like she's trying to figure something out. "It's a really nice trail," she says. That's all.

"Yeah. That's what he said. He—" I cut myself off, giving up less than halfway through my sentence.

Gemma takes over where I left off. "He's a good guy."

It's not much, but it's enough to open the door for me to ask for more. "How long have you guys known each other?"

She makes a little thinking face while she does some quick mental math. "Since I started here, so three years, give or take. At this point, we're close friends." She takes a breath before continuing. Here we go. "Listen, he's . . . he's been through a lot," she says. "And usually when he's up here, he's kind of a hermit. Honestly, it took me like a year of imposing myself before he let me anywhere near his house."

"Oh," I say, because my mind is reeling and I can't think of anything else. "That's . . . huh."

Gemma shrugs. "He'd be so annoyed if he knew I was talking about him like this. Jake really thinks he can take care of himself." She's smiling now, a fond, knowing look. Like he's a secret we're somehow both in on. I'm not sure she's right, but I like the idea of it.

VII

MAGGIE

After my conversation with Gemma, there's no way I'm going to refuse Jake's invitation. I text him and propose stopping by around eleven a.m., which seems like a good hour. Neutral. But friendly.

Then it's just a matter of keeping my heart rate in check as I slowly pass the next couple of hours. As I get dressed, get in my rental car, and guide it along winding, narrow roads toward his house.

When I pull into the driveway, I can see that it's smaller than I expected: not some strange modernist mansion or beautifully updated Victorian. Instead, he lives in a single-story A-frame, more low-key and cabin-like than anything at the Cabins. His truck is parked in the driveway, and I notice that there are no other, fancier cars in sight.

Most of what I see is evidence of the hobbies he's mentioned. A garage-turned-woodshop is visible around one side of the house. In front sit several raised beds, though it doesn't look like anything's been grown in them lately. The shape of a motorcycle hulks underneath a blue tarp, and I would bet good money that it just needs, like, three new parts to run perfectly again. A slew of projects on their way to completion. The overall effect is ramshackle but ultimately charming. Much like Jake.

I walk up to the front door, trying to keep my breath steady. Before I can even knock, I hear the sounds of a dog galloping across a wooden floor, followed by boot-heavy steps.

I've had plenty of time to prepare myself, but somehow I'm still not ready for Jake to greet me with that unbelievably disarming smile. He opens the door with one hand curled around the collar of a cattle mix who seems to want to say hello very, very badly.

"Hey," he says. "Sorry, I forgot to warn you about Buster. He's my neighbors', but he comes and hangs out with me sometimes when I'm in town. Isn't that right, Buster?" He looks directly at me. "Are you cool with dogs?"

"Very." Jake lets go of Buster's collar, and the next thing I know, I have paws on my stomach and a wet nose shoved in my chest. "Hey, hey," I say, gently pushing him down and bending to his level so we can introduce ourselves properly. "Hi, good boy."

"He's kind of a menace, actually. As you can see."

I glance up to where Jake is leaning against the doorframe, watching us with a faint smile. He's wearing a pair of threadbare, paint-stained jeans and a similarly filthy white Henley. He's also wearing the same shoes he had on at the Cabins, and yesterday at lunch: a pair of clunky, work-worn boots. My heart immediately clenches in my chest.

I rub behind Buster's ears. "All dogs are good dogs."

"Buster is a sweetheart," he allows. "But he's never in his life followed a rule. OK, *sit*."

Buster remains unseated. "Rules are overrated," I say. Buster seems satisfied by our interaction; he trots off to sniff things in the front yard, and I stand up. "Anyway. Hi."

"Hi." Jake's eyes flit down my body, like he can't help himself. I know Gemma seemed to imply earlier that I wasn't crazy to think there might be something between us. And Angela was all in, obviously. But with his gaze on me, that possibility goes from a horny theoretical to something all but likely. Every cell in me stands at attention in response.

"How's your morning been so far?" he asks.

"Good. It's been good," I say, like I don't trust myself right now with anything else.

"I'm glad. Here, I can show you how to get to the path."

I follow Jake down the steps, then toward the back of the property, where a field has been cleared. Beyond it is a seemingly endless stand of trees—birch, sugar maple, white pine. It's a bit past peak fall foliage, but they're glorious anyway, one final riot of crimson crowning their branches, like a fire against the blue of the sky.

"Wow" is somehow all I have to say.

Next to me, Jake just smiles. "It's pretty spectacular," he says. "One of the reasons I bought this place, honestly. It was right around this time of year the first time I saw it, and I thought if I could walk out of my front door to that view every day, it might end all my problems."

"And? Did it?"

Jake shakes his head. "There's a thing in AA called 'doing a geographic.' Your friend ever mention that one?"

"Nope."

"Well, it's basically the sobriety equivalent of *wherever you go, there you are.*"

"Still, this doesn't seem like the worst place in the world to be depressed."

That gets me a laugh. "It's not." Jake shoves his hands into his pockets, and I do my best not to fixate on the flex of his forearms. "And that's also not—I don't know. I do love being here. I think it makes me happier, more balanced."

"But," I say, thinking of running into Barbara yesterday and how easily it threw me for a loop, "you're still you?"

"Exactly." He points just ahead of us, where the field we've been walking through fades into trees again. "Anyway, this is it. If you're not back in a couple of hours, I'll send Buster. Then I'll call search and rescue."

"Good thing my friend Angela is tracking my location too." Whenever one of us goes on a Hinge date or travels somewhere with spotty cell service—say, to the isolated cabin of a guy we've only met twice—we text each other to say, *Here's when you can expect me back.* There are so many ways of being family that I didn't think about until I met her.

"Good to know someone's looking out for you." Instead of continuing our *Into the Wild* bit, he just gives me another dazzling smile. His hands are still in his pockets, and he almost looks bashful as he turns away to head back to the house.

I'm wearing a little crossbody bag, which has my earbuds in it. Like any New Yorker who's ever had a morning commute, they come everywhere with me. I'm tempted to pull them out and put on a podcast, or at least a playlist, but I decide to resist the temptation. I start down the path where it heads into the denser tree cover.

For the first time in a long while, I'm glad to be alone with my thoughts. Jake is right: The quiet here is somehow even thicker than it is at the Cabins. In part because it's not actually quiet, at least not when I really start to listen. I'm surrounded by the rustling of grass, whispering trees, crunching fallen leaves. Birds calling to each other, against the cracks and squeaks of squirrels playing in branches high above my head.

The path is pretty flat, and it's easy to fall into a soothing autopilot. My legs carry me steadily forward, but my mind drifts, thought after thought passing through my head like clouds. I should probably be using this time to contemplate My Future. Either this episode of burnout is an isolated incident—the expected consequence of being an entrepreneur in a capitalist society, et cetera—or a sign that I chose wrong and need to consider changing my life *again*.

But this is only my second real day of vacation. So instead of jumping to problem-solving, maybe I should actually try to just . . . be.

My brain goes in predictable directions, and I don't chastise myself. I think about some accounting stuff I want to check on when I get home. Revisit the question of Viola's hours again. I consider what I was doing when I was their age and whether they're ahead of me, or if I was ahead of them, and what "ahead" means, anyway.

But then I think about the built-ins Angela just had installed in her record store and the guy who did them and what elegant hands he had; he was in his sixties and not my type, but those *hands*—they really spoke to me. I think about the first guy I had a crush on, who I met at my grandparents' Upper Peninsula house. I think about the music I listened to that summer, and I hum an Elliot Smith song, adding my own noise to the muted cacophony around me.

I'm trying to remember the third verse when I emerge out of the trees to find the glistening edge of the lake. *Look at that*, I think; all I did was walk without worrying. And somehow, I've arrived.

VIII

JAKE

My original plan had been to spend the afternoon working. I had thought that maybe I could make good progress on the bookcase while Maggie hiked, and when she got back, I could mention that casually, and then maybe she'd want to see it. Maybe she'd be impressed, and I would immediately become a whole new person, or at least feel like one.

But as soon as I saw her with her hands buried in Buster's fur, I knew that a project that required my full attention was a lost cause. It wasn't remotely safe for me to pick up a power tool with my heart racing like that. So after I'd dropped her off at the trailhead, I went back to Perry Hill and grabbed a couple of sandwiches. In case she was hungry later.

That didn't take up nearly enough time, though, and I know I need to busy myself. I'm mostly used to the demands that sobriety makes of me, and I rarely miss the kind of partying I used to do. It's in small moments like these that I resent my inability to have just one drink—a single beer—to take the edge off. I don't keep social media on my phone, so escaping into some quality doomscrolling is out. I don't even smoke anymore. Instead, I have to just *feel* these feelings, and right now, all of them are at a manic simmer. I need to turn down the heat, so I grab my current knitting project from where it's waiting on the coffee table and sit down on the porch steps.

No one ever believes that I started knitting before I stopped drinking. In Mischief's early days, we had a sort of "Tour Mom"—something like a manager, if a manager also wrangled the interpersonal dramas of four guys in their late teens who had suddenly gotten extraordinarily famous and wealthy. She was a woman in her fifties named Alberta. Flight delays, overnight bus rides, and endless waits in venue dressing rooms were always accompanied by the click-clack of her needles. She taught me the basics during a vicious bout of jet lag while we were touring in Asia, and I kept it up the whole time I was in the band. It was how I passed time when I wasn't drunk or high: knitting scarves that got Lenny Kravitz–large before I finally wised up and just started making huge blankets instead.

This particular one is made from local wool; it's been dyed a deep red with beetroot. It still smells faintly of sheep, which I find comforting—though it means I do have to keep Buster from getting too interested. Finally, he settles down at my feet for a nap.

I'm so immersed in the blanket that I don't see Maggie emerging from the tree line. It's Buster who picks up her scent, even in his sleep. His eyes stay closed, but his ears prick up, and he whines softly, the sound he makes when he's curious about something. By the time I look up to see what he's reacting to, she's close enough that I can see her smiling. And not just smiling, but smiling at me.

It's too late to hide what I've been up to, so I put the project down as Maggie walks up to the front steps, one hand shading her eyes from the sun. "Hey," she says. "Are you knitting?"

"I was."

She grins. Her cheeks are pink, and her hair is piled on top of her head. "I see. Well. You were right. That was really special."

"I'm glad."

There's a pause where I can almost see her weighing whether it's time to go or not. But then she says, "Can I ask what you're working on?"

"Just a blanket."

"For yourself, or . . ."

"Not for me. I have so many. Actually, now pretty much everyone I know has one. Do you need a blanket by any chance?"

Maggie laughs. "You must love knitting."

"I do, actually," I say. I stand up, leaning against one of the porch pillars, my shoulder pressing against the light wood. "The problem is that I don't really care what I make. Some people always want to try a new project or technique, but for me, it's just the act of doing the thing."

"Process over product." She looks over at what I've got so far. "I like the color. Same as my favorite ranunculus."

"It really is yours if you want it. Speaking of which—I

went by Perry Hill to grab a sandwich, and I figured I'd pick one up for you too. No pressure, though. I can always save it if you've got plans."

"I was actually just thinking about how hungry I was." Maggie switches the hand that's been shading her eyes, and I notice that her nails are short and bare. Like she keeps her hands busy too, but doing actually useful things.

I look back to her face, and I see the anticipation there. This is, of course, exactly what I hoped would happen. I just can't believe that it actually did. "Well, I was about to eat mine. If you want to join me."

"That would be nice." Maggie climbs the stairs to the porch, and Buster rises to greet her. I open the door to let the three of us in.

It's immediately surreal. Almost no one has ever been inside this place. My neighbors visit, but they only stop by briefly. Gemma has spent a few afternoons on the property, keeping me company on days when it felt like the world was closing in around me like a fist. But really, I'm almost always here alone.

The sight of Maggie walking into my living room nearly undoes me. The space is small: The living room opens onto a kitchen, with a breakfast nook off to one side. On the other side is the bathroom and my bedroom. There's not much of a house to tour.

But Maggie still takes it in: the piles of blankets—I wasn't kidding about the blankets—covering the worn-in couch and the art on the walls, which is mostly stuff from local artists I've picked up over the years. A mug left from my pottery phase sits on the kitchen counter, still half-full of this morning's drip coffee, but otherwise, the surface is almost completely bare. For all the skills I've picked up over the years, cooking has not yet been one of them.

I grab us plates and napkins, and Buster knows his cue to settle under the table and see if any scraps fall his way.

"Do you want water?" I ask. "Coffee? I think that's all I've got. Oh, and Diet Coke."

Maggie fights a smile.

"What?"

"Just that Diet Coke doesn't really fit the vibe of this place."

"I have to drive to Woodstock to get it," I admit. "It's my one remaining addiction. I've quit booze, drugs, and nicotine, but aspartame? It's got me in a chokehold."

"I hate to be the bad influence here, but I would love a Diet Coke."

"In that case, I'll join you."

The breakfast nook is on the western side of the house, and it's flooded with afternoon light as we settle into our seats. We each crack our cans open, and Maggie holds hers up for a toast.

"Cheers," she says. Then after a moment's consideration: "To vacation friends."

I hold up my own Diet Coke to clink against hers. "So," I say. "Did you appreciate the foliage out there? Get any ideas for new arrangements or anything?"

Maggie shakes her head. "I managed not to think about work much, actually."

"Oh, sorry. We don't have to talk about it."

She waves her hand not holding the sandwich. "No, it's fine. It's not off-limits or anything. But it was nice to just . . . take a break."

"You said yesterday that it's pretty intense."

"And that it's intense because I make it that way." Maggie sighs and unwraps her sandwich. I watch her take a bite, chew, and swallow before continuing. "When I was working in finance, arranging flowers was my happy place. The way I relaxed when work was making me nuts. Now it *is* the work. And sometimes it feels like . . . why did I have to go and ruin my favorite thing like that? Lately I can't see a bouquet without calculating how much each stem cost and thinking about where each one came from. Wondering if the person who put it together charges more than I do, if they have a better work-life balance, and . . ." She shakes her head. "I need to make it fun again, but I have no idea how."

"Mischief got to be that way. At the end. Or maybe earlier, I don't know."

Maggie leans forward slightly, propping her elbows on the table. "Do you still make music?" she asks.

"Nope. I like to sing, and I can play decent guitar, so I'll do that sometimes. But I was never a songwriter. That's really Charlie's thing."

"Do you miss any of it, though?"

I rub a hand over my face. "What a question."

"You don't have to—"

"No, no, it's fine, it's just—" It's impossible to answer, is what it is. I miss the adrenaline rush of performing. I miss how it felt to hear our voices all mixing together. But I don't miss the insecurity that dogged me every minute I was offstage. How I used the crowd's adulation to try to mask how I felt inside, which was all too often miserable. How, despite the misery, I was probably as addicted to every part of the celebrity as I was to alcohol.

Charlie seems to be able to separate all of that out: to figure out the difference between the way fame was thrust upon us when we were teenagers and what it means to choose notoriety for himself now. He loves music enough to do that, but this time on his terms. He has been able to hold on to the creativity, let that fuel him. For me, the whole thing still feels like a tangle that's best left alone. "I miss it," I say. "And I also don't think I ever need to do it again."

Maggie not-very-sneakily passes Buster a scrap of chicken from her sandwich. "So what do you do, then? When you're not knitting. Or out here trying to learn carpentry."

Another good question. That I don't really have an answer to. "I have the opposite problem that you do, I think," I say. "I don't have a job. I don't really . . . need to have one. I travel a lot. Meet people. Try things." I shrug. "I think you were right. It's all a vacation."

"Nonstop fun," she says. But her tone doesn't match the words.

My gaze catches on Maggie's, and I find I can't look away. The flush in her cheeks has faded, but her mouth is still so red. "It should be. Fun," I say. "But lately it all feels the same, no matter what I do. So I've been thinking that maybe I should, you know, try committing to something instead."

She's mostly finished her sandwich, and she runs a fingertip along her plate, collecting stray crumbs. "Is that what you want, though?" she asks.

The light through the window keeps moving; now it's slicing across Maggie's face, making her warm-brown eyes glow golden. There's a helpless honesty that overtakes me in her presence, it seems. "I think I do."

Whatever she's about to say is cut off by a knock coming from the front of the house. Maggie and I both startle, and Buster's head pops up from under the table. He must have been sleeping; he sniffs the air and starts trotting toward the door. "That's probably Isaiah," I say. "His owner. Sometimes they need him for—"

"Jake," Isaiah calls from the porch. "You got Buster in there?"

"Sure do," I yell back. I get up and go to unbolt the door—a locked door is a city habit I'll probably never be able to break.

Isaiah came to get Buster but also to ask if I can take him again while they're away this weekend. Though I'm happy to, I don't want to talk details right now, and my ears prick at the sounds of Maggie moving around in the kitchen. Probably gathering her things. Getting ready to leave. By the time I've said goodbye to Isaiah, she's just behind me, her bag looped over her shoulder again. "I should," she says, gesturing toward the door.

I want to try to delay her exit, but I don't. She has her

day to get back to. A vacation of her own. Then a life that doesn't involve me.

"Yeah," I say. "Of course. Well. It was good to see you again."

"It was good to see you too." She flushes just barely this time, a sweet, pale pink. "Thanks again for—for everything."

"Of course."

I know what should happen here. I should tell Maggie that I want to see her again. Because I do very much want to see her again. But I'm out of practice at taking real risks, and I freeze. I can feel my smile becoming a rictus. I should at least try to give her a hug, I think, but my body won't move.

I don't know what Maggie sees when she looks at me at this moment. But she pauses. And then she reaches up and wraps her arms around me. I duck my head into her embrace, and she brushes her lips against my cheek.

It's such a tiny kiss. Almost nothing. As I'm turning into her, she's already pulling away, her skin now singed bright red. "OK," she says. "OK, I mean, goodbye, and see you soon, or—yeah."

Now I have to say something. To tell her to stay. To tell her literally anything. But all those words remain locked up in my chest. Instead, I stand there like an idiot as she hurries down the stairs to her car.

IX

MAGGIE

The first thing I do when I get back to the Cabins is pop a weed gummy in an attempt to try to erase my racing thoughts. *What the hell was that?* It would have been one thing to really make a move. Just put it all out there and see what happened. Instead, I kissed Jake on the cheek, like a grandmother. And when he lingered in response, I pulled back and fled the scene.

It's just that, in the moment, it felt like the only thing I could do. His hands looked so empty, standing there: Buster had gone; I was about to be gone too. I wanted to fill the space around him. I wanted to touch him carefully, to drag it out. I wanted . . .

That's as far as I get before the gummy starts to kick in. For most of the rest of the day, all I can do is sit in the grass near the lake, watching the sun shimmer on the water, letting it burn afterimages onto the insides of my eyelids. I text Angela, *what did I do*, and she writes back, *I don't know? What did you do???*

But I don't respond. Instead, I wait and watch as the

high crests, peaks, and then slowly starts to leave me, going out as inevitably as a tide.

What did I do? I met a man; we had a couple of nice conversations. I kissed his cheek. It all adds up to barely anything.

But I wanted it to be more. After years of subsuming my passion into my work, I'm remembering what it feels like to experience pure, uncut *want* again. To desire just for the hell of it. To let that lead me instead of parceling my life up into Google Calendar boxes and doling it out an hour at a time.

And to have no idea if it will amount to anything.

As the sun starts to set, I make my way back to my cabin. I remember I left Angela hanging. I text her, *sorry got a little too high, ignore me.* Then I put my phone down and pace around the space, trailing my hands over surfaces, feeling their textures against my fingertips.

Ever since I've been here, I've felt unusually aware of my body: My skin buffeted by the wind while I rode that bike yesterday. The chill in my veins when I dipped my toes in the lake during my hike today. Everything in me going aflame every time Jake's gaze catches on mine.

And being stoned pulls me to linger longer, unabashedly, on that last thought. I press a palm against the smooth wood of the walls, the curve of a vase, the white cotton flannel of my bedsheets. Then an idea occurs to me. I go to my bag and pull out a small, as-yet-unopened box.

Maybe this will take the edge off, I think as I unwrap my new vibrator. A good orgasm could clear my head. Who knows? Maybe it's not Jake so much as it is that I am garden-variety horny.

I strip off my clothes and slip under the covers. It feels weird to be so intentional. Usually at home when I masturbate, it's a quick hit: a response to some random flash of desire. Now I slide a hand across my stomach, palming the softness while a much more visceral desire pulses through me.

There's no point in doing things halfway, I think. I close my eyes and allow myself to imagine Jake's hand sliding across my navel. His face dipping to press against my neck. His voice, husky with want, murmuring my name.

The rest of the fantasy comes easy now, thick and vivid. I can almost feel the press of his chest against mine, the satisfying weight of him between my legs. A little noise escapes my throat. I suck my fingertips and stroke their wetness against my own. *I've missed this*, I think: exploring my body just for the hell of it. Feeling the pleasure bloom inside of me, taking its time.

When I want more than my own hand can give, I reach for the vibrator and thumb it on. I'm already swollen and sensitive, and I gasp when it starts to flutter against me. Then, with no one around to hear me, I let out a moan. I use a free hand to play with one nipple, pinching it with the pulse of the vibrations. The pain pricks, and pleasure spreads, expands. Unconsciously, I grip my thighs tight around the toy, riding it like it's him. I imagine him fucking me, his hands on my ass, in my mouth, and though my mind could go on, that's it for my body: I'm shaking and swearing and coming, hips bucking mindlessly with release.

As my orgasm subsides, I press my face into the pillow and try to breathe. I realize I'm not any less on edge. I feel like a steam room. Somehow I'm filling and filling with more want, more desire. It's clouding every other thought.

I flash back to a room very much like this one, ten years ago, probably almost to the day. The last time I went on a fancy vacation, that time to the Bahamas. I was with my then-boyfriend Zach, a Goldman coworker with a sly sense of humor and boundless ambition. We went away for four nights and fucked on exactly one of them: the kind of fine-but-perfunctory sex it's easy to slide into with someone you aren't that into anymore.

I remember lying in bed the next morning, blanketed by the despair that came over me when I realized that I couldn't be with this man for another month, much less the rest of my life. I felt like I had everything else figured out: flashy degree, dream apartment, excellent job. I had just needed a handsome husband on equal footing to complete the picture.

Instead, I knocked the canvas off the easel. Quit the job, moved out, remade my life. And whatever happens after—even if I shut down my business or who knows what—it will have been worth it. It will have been worth it to try to let desire dictate my life instead of falling into dull convention.

Now I just need to get back to the want that started it all.

I can still smell my own sex on my fingertips when I fumble my phone into my hands and open up the text thread with Jake. It's a sparse few messages, completely utilitarian: me suggesting a time earlier this morning, and him sharing his address a little while later. But we talked, really talked, yesterday and then again today. We talked like people talk when they're getting to know each other and are willing to dig below the surface. When they're interested in knowing more.

Do you ever feel like it's actually TOO dark here? I text. *I'm having trouble falling asleep without that ambient city glow.* He can ignore it if he wants.

A few minutes later, Jake writes back, *all the time*. And then: *Don't tell my therapist, but I listen to podcasts to fall asleep sometimes.*

Does that work? I ask.

Sure, if you can get over how depressing it is, he replies.

What's depressing is that I'm sore from a bike ride and a hike. I need to get out more.

There's a pause almost long enough to make me nervous. But then he replies, *Have you not explored the Cabins' spa menu?*

The very luxe soaking tubs are all booked. Turns out not everything here can be on a whim.

Another lapse follows. I'm about to put my phone down when bubbles pop up to indicate that Jake is typing.

He replies, *Well, you're welcome to use mine.*

I have to reread his text three times before I'm sure it says what I think it says. What I *want* it to say. Then there are more typing bubbles, but this time, they disappear without him actually sending anything else.

I loll my head back on the pillow, staring at the ceiling for a long moment. This is happening. This is—it has to be happening. The door has swung wide open.

I'm going to walk through it.

I would take you up on that, I say.

Come by tomorrow, if you want, Jake writes back.

WEDNESDAY

X

JAKE

After coffee the next morning, I put on my running clothes. It's cold enough that I need to layer up: tights, shorts, a long sleeve, and a windbreaker on top. I add a beanie and throw my phone in my stupid little fanny pack. It looks so dumb, but it came with a water bottle attachment that keeps my hands free, and, anyway, there's usually no one else on the roads here, so who cares.

I learned early on in my recovery that running could burn the energy that always needs an outlet and that it travels well. I can do it anywhere. I've run marathons in New York, Sydney, and London. I've also run tens of thousands of miles on the roads near this house, the pound of my feet wiping my mind blank and pushing me as close as I've ever come to meditating.

This morning, though, it's like my shoes beat out *Maggie, Maggie, Maggie* against the asphalt.

Maggie's not just coming over. She's coming over with intention. Ever since I met her, I've been feeling like the two of us are subject to a gravitational pull: a force tugging me gently, inevitably into her orbit.

I should be ecstatic. Instead, I'm panicking. It feels like I felt the first time I had to go on a date completely sober: ripped open, exposed, and vulnerable. If this happens, there won't be any pretending that it doesn't mean something. She's not someone who plays around. She takes herself seriously, and for some reason, it seems like she takes me seriously too.

It's like the universe was saying, *You wanted something more meaningful than what you've had? Here it is, Ramsey. Don't fuck it up!*

In theory, I should have the tools for this. Twelve years of sobriety. Time in the rooms, with a therapist, with the people in my life, working on repair and forgiveness. Plenty of experience with women. In reality, though, this feels like a level up. One I'm not at all sure I'm ready for.

I find myself pushing my pace, running my third and fourth miles faster than one and two. I'm halfway through a fifth when I realize I probably should have turned around ten minutes ago. I head back, and the run home is fast enough that I don't have time to think about anything except for avoiding tripping over stray rocks. I make it just in time to jog up the driveway alongside Maggie's rental car.

I toss the fanny pack and windbreaker onto the porch while she's getting out of her car. There's no way to avoid looking sweaty, but at least I can look slightly less dorky.

"Hey," Maggie says. "Am I early? I can come back, if—"

"No," I assure her. "I'm just running late."

She smirks. "Literally." And then, when I don't respond, she points at me as if to remind me of my logged miles.

"Oh, I got it. I just didn't think it was that funny," I tease.

Maggie puts her hands on her hips as if she's about to argue, but after a second, she drops them. "Honestly, fair."

I just like her so much. "Want to come in? I'll grab you a towel."

We climb the steps together, and I realize that inviting Maggie inside my house is starting to feel familiar. She's wearing a long-sleeve shirt and a pair of baggy sweatpants that only make me more aware that she'll be soon removing them. "How've you been?" I ask, mostly in an attempt to distract myself from the thought.

From the edge of my vision, I think I catch her blushing. "Fine," she says, maybe a little too quickly. "You know, I hate to say this, but if I hadn't met you, I think I might be a little bored."

I head to the linen closet. "Isn't the point of this vacation to relax?" I call over one shoulder.

Maggie has one hip leaning up against the kitchen counter. "The point," she says, "is to do whatever I want."

I'm glad I'm turned away from her so she can't see what happens to my body when I hear her say that.

When I come back into the kitchen and hand Maggie the towel, she looks down at it like she's confused, and then back up at me. "Oh," she says. "You're not joining me?"

The world tilts, just slightly, on its axis. This is happening. This is actually happening. "I didn't want to presume," I say. "Only if you want."

Maggie looks nervous, which is honestly a relief. "I," she starts. "I want."

I feel those two words all the way down to my marrow.

"I'll change," I say. I go to my room, where it's a relief to strip off my sweaty running clothes. I pull on swim trunks and a sweatshirt and grab a towel for myself, trying to move quickly to keep my racing mind from getting in the way. Then I lead Maggie out the back door, my fingertips hovering over her lower back.

The hot tub is in a clearing in the middle of a stand of trees. It's not as nice as the Cabins'—just a prefab thing I picked up a couple of years ago. But there's something decadent about it anyway: being nearly naked and warm in the middle of the cold woods.

I left the cover on when I turned the heat on earlier; now I hoist it off and watch as steam rises from the water. Maggie and I both put our towels on the little ledge next to the tub. As I tug my sweatshirt off, I feel her eyes on me, and I don't try to hide the smile at the corners of my mouth.

I'm in very good shape—the running does its job, as do the weights I have set up in my garage—but my body still reveals a lot about who I am and where I've been that I hope I'm ready for her to see. I have stupid tattoos from my drinking days: an anchor on my ribs, a piece of rope knotted around one bicep. My chest hair is turning gray, and there's a light scar across my stomach from my teenage appendectomy. My body bears the marks of the realities of my forty-two years.

Maggie was faster than me, somehow, and when I look

up, she's already climbing the steps to the hot tub and starting to slide into the water. I catch glimpses of the curves of her thighs and the high, round swell of her ass. Her deep-berry suit is cut low enough in the front to make me equal parts dismayed and grateful when her cleavage disappears beneath the surface.

I join her, and for a few moments, we just sit. We're silent, but it's somehow not awkward. Maggie's cheeks go pink, and her mouth reddens. She's pulled her hair up into a loose bun, but a curl escapes at the nape of her neck.

"So did you finish your blanket?" she asks after a little while. "Or the bookcase?"

I shake my head. "Haven't touched the bookshelf lately."

"Why not?"

I shrug. "I'm better at working on things than finishing them."

Maggie reaches out to nudge me with one foot. It's just her sole on my calf, but the contact still makes my body sing. "Why do I get the sense that this cabin is where you come to hide out from your problems?" she asks.

I dramatically clutch my hands against my heart. "Ow! A direct hit."

"You don't exactly make a secret of it."

"It's just—" I make myself look at her. "You just—this is just kind of a weird time in my life."

"What's making it so weird?"

"A lot of things," I say. And then I realize that I feel compelled to give her specifics. "My breakup, for one."

"Still licking your wounds?" she asks gently.

That would be the sob-appropriate story: that I'm brokenhearted and maybe in need of a rebound. But I'm feeling too much for Maggie already not to show her the whole, ugly truth. To let her decide what to do with it. "It's the opposite, actually," I confess. "I'm not heartbroken, and I feel awful about it. Like, I dated Kelsey for almost a year. I met her parents. She was great. She was wonderful, even. There was absolutely nothing wrong with her. I know I should feel worse about it. But I just . . . don't."

I expect Maggie to recoil, grimace, pull back in some way. Instead, she nods. "*There's nothing wrong with her* isn't really a good reason to be with someone though. By that metric, I should still be with my last ex too."

I look down at the bubbles on the tub's surface, then back at her. "There really wasn't *anything* wrong with him?"

"I mean, of course he was annoying sometimes. He did that thing where, when he talked to people with accents, he would unconsciously start imitating how they talked back at them, which he wasn't doing on purpose, but it was still *so* embarrassing to witness. And he was obsessed with knowing the size of the annual bonus of everyone he worked with." She shrugs, and I watch the water move around her body. Trying not to look at her actual body is a battle I'm slowly, steadily losing. "But ultimately, no, there wasn't anything *wrong* with him in a meaningful way. That's not what ended it."

I lean in a little closer. So close I can smell her: woodsmoke and tuberose, her perfume or shampoo beading up in her sweat. "And what was that?"

Maggie holds my gaze. "I didn't want him enough to stick around and make it work. I mean, at a certain point, it's just chemistry, isn't it?"

I know exactly what she means. But I've been betrayed by the pull of my own desires for most of my life. Gripped by the things I wanted that didn't serve me—alcohol, fame. This chemical tug toward Maggie feels different, though.

"And you trusted that," I say, trying to keep my voice steady. "That you could pursue what you wanted. That you could trust *yourself*."

Maggie presses a palm against the side of her neck, runs it upward, and threads her fingers through her hair. She's looking at me through half-lidded eyes, and a pang goes through me, sudden and sharp. The ease of our conversation gives way to sparks of something deeper, threatening to catch. "I don't always trust myself," she says. "But I do have trouble not going after what I want."

I want. Those words echo in my ears, overlapping with how she responded when I asked if I could join her earlier, and I move before I can even really think. In a blur, I cross the hot tub to her and lift her so she's sitting on the ledge. I stand between her knees, water streaming down both of our bodies, steam rising from our skin. "This is what I want," I murmur.

"Good," she says, draping her arm over my shoulders and tilting her mouth up toward mine. "Me too."

I've been thinking so much these past few days, overthinking maybe, but it's freeing to release my brain's hold on me and be powerless against desire. It feels so good to give in: to follow the instinctual pull of my body to hers. I want my hands on her ass, so I slide them there, digging my fingers into her flesh. Her lips part, and I press my mouth against hers, finally. It's as warm as the water around us. I urge her hips against my torso, soft against hard, and we both gasp at the contact.

We're moving quickly, too close to naked. When she spreads her knees wider and arches her back, my base impulse is to pull her bathing suit aside and fuck her right here, out in the open. It's somehow not enough to hear her whine as I trail kisses along the line of her throat, to feel her melt when I tug down her shoulder straps so I can get my mouth on her breasts. I want to claim her. I want to fill her up until she's as full of me as I feel of her.

But I need to preserve some tiny shred of sanity. So instead, I kneel on the tub's bench between her legs, kissing the tender insides of her thighs. I look up at her, tugging her bathing suit the rest of the way. Once she realizes what's happening, she stands and helps, shimmying the fabric off and letting it drift away in the water. I have to stop and stare. To let my eyes trace the arcs of her naked form and fall to the soft tuft marking the place I want her most.

Maggie sits back down, slowly spreading her legs and locking eyes for my reaction. I can't help but let out a low groan. She gives a satisfied smile and leans back on her hands.

I lick up the side of her stomach and across the crease where her hip meets her thigh. She tugs her hair loose and lets it fall behind her as her head drops. When I get my mouth on her, she gasps, and her thighs tighten against my shoulders. I hold her open, drawing my tongue through her salty, musky sweetness. I try to read her rhythm, noticing when she pulls me closer by my hair, hissing out a breath, and when she eases me away, drawing out her pleasure. I want to see just how much I can wring out of her. "Tell me how you want it, Maggie," I say with my lips pressed to her clit.

"Slow," she says. "Wet."

Jesus. I flatten my tongue against her, and I don't know that I've ever wanted anything like I want this woman to come on my mouth. To know that she wanted something and I gave it to her.

She doesn't have to tell me when she's getting close; I can feel her breathing pick up, her limbs becoming overwhelmed. Her head rolls back as her orgasm crashes over both of us; I grasp her close, offering no relief and loving how it feels when she squirms against me, riding the edge of *too much*. Of letting me give that to her.

XI

MAGGIE

There's a moment where I think I might never stop coming; maybe I'll just spend the rest of my life riding the flat of Jake's tongue, my body and brain reduced to helpless pulses of pleasure. But eventually, my body stills, my brain comes back online, and more rational thoughts slowly creep back.

I have to unclench my fingers from where they're tightly threaded through Jake's hair. I've gotten cold, sitting naked in the fall air, and I slip back into the warm water and twist my hair up off my neck again. Jake slides down the bench to make room for me and leaves space between us, watching me like I'm going to take it back. Or maybe like he doesn't trust himself to sit too close.

"Jesus, Jake," I sigh, spreading my arms across the rim of the tub, my fingers still inches from his shoulder.

He laughs, relieved. Pleased with himself.

We sit there for a moment, with matching grins, recovering.

I close my eyes and breathe in the chill in the air. "Thank you for indulging me."

Jake's laugh pierces the tranquility of the scene. A chipmunk or a squirrel scurries. "Oh, is that what that was?"

I nod, my eyes still closed. Jake laughs, and I open them to watch him. His mouth is flushed, and I go hot all over again, remembering how it got that way.

I shift closer to him and drag my fingers up his shoulder and along his neck. Jake looks surprised, and for a horrifying moment, I wonder whether this was a one-time thing. If he's not turned on right now. But then he bites his lower lip and shifts his hips in that telltale *I don't know what to do about my boner* way.

He sees me notice, and his eyes widen. "I'm fine," he says. "You don't have to."

I stand, feeling deeply self-satisfied at the expression on Jake's face as he watches me slide myself onto his lap, my knees bracketing his hips. Given how talented I've discovered his mouth to be, I'm now very interested in his dick. "What did I say," I ask, "about going after what I want?"

"Fuck, Maggie," he groans as I press down onto him. Whatever mind games he's playing with himself, whatever sort of gentleman he's trying to be, his body knows exactly what it needs. His arms pull me closer, so that his hardness is trapped between us.

"You're fine? You're sure you don't want me to do something about this?" I ask. I lick my lips, knowing exactly what I'm doing.

Whatever self-control has been pinning him down finally cracks. "Of *course* I want you to touch me," he rumbles, his eyes unable to meet mine. "And I've wanted you to touch me since—" He stops.

"Since when?" I prompt. "Was it when I scarfed a sandwich in front of you at Perry Hill? Or when I showed up here in my hiking boots? Or—"

"The second I saw you," he says, finally looking up at me. "In the hotel lobby. How flushed you got when I ran into you. Your hair. Maggie, your mouth—" And then he pulls me down for a kiss.

I had a vision: Making Jake and his hard-on walk back down the path to his house. Getting a condom and fucking him senseless. But I reach down to pull him out of his swim trunks, and he feels so big in my hand, his cock just as hungry for attention as his mouth. We're wrapped in this moment, and I can't deny either of us the pleasure of just letting things unfold. My grip is slippery, and I work my hand over him, shifting back and forth with my hips, as I claw my other hand through his hair, curling in the dampness. I want him to feel just as exposed and overwhelmed and undone as I did, when my gasps echoed through the trees with no one to hear them but us.

His head is tilted back, and I'm judging his closeness by his murmurs and the sweat accumulating across this throat. His breath goes ragged as I work him to the edge. But just as he gets there, his brain clicks on, and he remembers something. He looks at me, pupils blown, eyes desperate, thrusting up into my hand on every stroke. "Oh, god, I can't come in the hot tub," he says, panting. "It's a bitch to clean, seriously, *seriously*—"

"OK, OK, let me—"

Jake helps me out of his lap, and we try to stand up together, but we're an awkward tangle of limbs. He groans, desperate to get out and get off, and he hurries to the lawn, jerking himself off onto the grass. He starts laughing, and then we're both naked and cracking up at the absurdity of all of this.

"You really are bad at finishing things," I say, unblinking.

He presses a fist to his forehead and chuckles harder, soundlessly. "OK, that—that was funny. I take hot tub maintenance really seriously," he says, still breathing heavily.

I hand him a towel, tears of laughter still in my eyes. "I'm taking it as a compliment. You were quite distracted."

Jake raises an eyebrow, smirking at my nakedness as I wrap myself in a towel "You were—" He pauses. "Very distracting."

"Good."

I grab my discarded bathing suit and the rest of my clothes, jamming my feet into my sneakers.

"You could rinse off inside, if you want."

"That would be great, thank you."

We make our way back through the trees, and Jake shows me the shower. I turn it on and let the small room fill with steam. I could use a moment to digest everything that just happened. That was so good. But surprisingly intense.

Or maybe I shouldn't be surprised. We've had chemistry since the moment we met.

This is a good thing, I remind myself as I step under the spray. I don't need to spiral out into any potential futures. I just had the best sex I've had in ages and pursued a level of desire I didn't even consider possible when I started this trip. It doesn't need to be any deeper than that.

I dry off and get dressed again. When I emerge, Jake is wearing what has to be the sexiest pair of gray sweats I've ever seen, or perhaps it's the still-raging endorphins talking. He's leaning against the kitchen counter, cradling a mug. "Good shower?" he asks.

"Good shower," I nod.

I want to walk over and press myself up against him. Kiss him again and then again. But I don't know whether that's permissible, what our arrangement is, so I stay rooted to the spot.

"I just want to tell you," Jake says after a long minute of us just standing there. "I didn't expect—I didn't expect anything when I invited you over. I mean, I *wanted* you. I wanted to fuck you—"

"I was hoping," I say. "When you invited me over."

The smile he returns is sweet, almost shy. He glances past me, to the living room. "Do you want to maybe stay for a minute? I made a pot of tea. But I understand if you need to get back."

"I'd love some tea."

We curl up on opposite ends of his couch, one of his hand-knit blankets thrown over my bare feet. Jake is looking at me like he can't quite believe I'm still here.

"I was sort of hoping I'd get to see Buster again," I admit.

"Me too," Jake says. "But he's on his own schedule. I never know when he's going to stop by, or how long he's going to stay."

"You have to respect that." I twist the wool between my fingers. "Do you ever think about getting a dog of your own?"

Jake shakes his head. "When I'm out here it's perfect, but the rest of the time . . . I'd hate to have to use a kennel that often. I travel way too much. And I know people have dogs in the city, but they always look kind of miserable. It just doesn't feel fair."

"Depends on the dog. My friend Angela—her dog is on a first-name basis with the local butcher. Gets grass-fed organic bones saved for him on the daily. I don't think he'd trade city living for anything."

"That does sound like a pretty good setup."

I straighten my legs, and Jake does the same. Our calves brush, and Jake slouches into the cushions, leaning into the contact. "So what are you going to do with the rest of your time here?" he asks. "I really have shown you everything I've got at this point."

I run my gaze over his body performatively. "You sure have."

Jake rolls his eyes, but he looks smug about it.

"I'm only here for a couple more days, actually," I say. It feels wrong to acknowledge reality in this moment that feels so suspended in time. *But that's why I have to do it*, I think. In order to pin myself to something more solid than the cloud I've been floating on all afternoon. "Till Saturday morning. Tomorrow night I'm having dinner at Basket." The restaurant at the Cabins is a whole thing—it's made all the best-of lists ever since the new chef took it over a few years ago. There are people who will make the drive up here just for dinner.

"You know, I've never been," Jake says. "I know Tarik, and I've eaten at the bar so many times. But getting a table at Basket is such a thing, so I always kind of figure I'll do it at some point, and just never have."

As if the man couldn't make a call on any night and get a table.

Maybe the reality I just broached hasn't quite set in yet, or maybe it's the concreteness of my short timeline that has me feeling bold. "Why don't you come with me?"

"To dinner?" Jake tilts his chin.

"To dinner," I say. "They're going to seat me at a two-top anyway, right? You might have plans or something. Just an idea." My brain has finally caught up with my mouth, and I can barely meet Jake's gaze as I stammer. I take a long gulp of my tea just to shut myself up.

For a moment, Jake seems to be wrestling with something, and I'm reeling too. Sure, it's fun to hook up on vacation, but now I'm roping him into a proper date. I flex my toes into the weave of the blanket as I wait. His face clears. "I would like that," he says, knocking his leg against mine. "What time?"

XII

JAKE

It's fine, I tell myself. She's here for two more days. It doesn't have to be that big of a deal. I go on dates all the time. I've been in relationships that have lasted a year (barely, but still). I don't know why I'm letting myself make dinner with a woman who is here on vacation for a week feel high stakes. Like it matters that she asks me real questions and somehow gets me to give real answers. That I've been more open with her than maybe anyone besides Gemma.

Because no matter what happens at dinner, on Saturday, Maggie will go back to the city, and a few days later, I'll head off to Berlin. This will end before I have time to fuck it up and prove to myself that I can't do this after all. Instead, I can enjoy Maggie while she's here and let her go when she goes.

All I have to do is remember that, and I'll be fine.

THURSDAY

XIII

MAGGIE

The promise of our upcoming dinner gives my Thursday shape. The weather is glorious—once again crisp, but sunny—and after I do an hour of yoga, I take a long walk through the Cabins' big garden. It's impossible not to think about my work amid the marigolds, asters, and evening primrose, but the thoughts are abstract enough that their presence is soothing. I touch velvety petals and wonder what it would be like to make a bouquet of textures; I consider that I love the look of seed heads and should do more with them. It's a reminder of what drew me to this job, before I really had it: the pure aesthetic joy of working with living things.

I have a massage booked for the late afternoon, and by the time I get back to my hotel room in the early evening, I'm fully enveloped in a cocoon of deep relaxation. Right now, it's easy to pretend that I'll get to keep living this way indefinitely, that my departure isn't just around the corner.

I deliberately push that thought out of my mind as I start to get ready for dinner, taking extra time with my hair and rummaging through my toiletries for the chocolate-brown eyeliner I only wear when I'm really getting dressed up. Jake has already seen me naked, but part of me is still anxious.

There's no question of what I'll wear. I brought one of my favorite dresses, which I bought a couple of years ago as a *fuck it* present for myself: an acknowledgment that I wasn't going to fight the softening of my body anymore. As I'd gotten older, I tried to stave off the inevitable with ramped-up exercise and increasingly restrictive diets; turns out, the only thing I succeeded in doing was making myself miserable. This purchase was me saying I was just going to let my body do its thing.

The dress is simple: a low-backed swath of black jersey from Helmut Lang that flatters my curves. It's also comfortable. No amount of indulging tonight will leave me feeling regretful.

I'm ready a little too early, and I consider another session with the vibrator just to take the edge off, to get me out of my head. But I find that I like the idea of dragging out the anticipation. Spending all of dinner horny and excited for the possibilities of afterward: one hunger being sated while another one learns some patience.

I head toward Basket, following lanterns that line the path. The restaurant is about a ten-minute walk away; it's freestanding, tucked at the easternmost corner of the property and atop of a gentle rise in the land, overlooking the lake. I can feel my cheeks going pink in the cold and then immediately glowing red when I walk into its warmth.

When I spot Jake leaning against the host stand and chatting easily with the hostess, my flush somehow deepens—I feel the burning in my cheeks and up to my hairline. He's dressed simply too, in a white button-down and a pair of crisp black pants. Before I can say anything, he turns around. His gaze runs over me, and the look on his face makes every scrap of self-doubt vanish. "Maggie," he says softly enough so only I can hear.

I do like hearing him say my name.

Jake's shirt is open at the collar, and I really had been planning on being circumspect—letting him take the lead tonight, after being the one who proposed the date—but I can't resist stepping in to hug him and discretely pressing my nose against the exposed skin at the hollow of his throat. He's not wearing cologne, but he still smells insanely good, just the pure musk of his skin. I step back, and Jake snakes his arm around my waist, a proprietary palm resting gently on my back.

God, we haven't gotten to our table yet, and I'm already wet.

The hostess smirks at Jake in a way that indicates that she's amused—maybe even delighted—to see him in this mode. "Are you ready to be seated?" she asks with a grin.

We nod in unison, and she leads us to a small, extra private table with a sweeping view of the lake. The moon is full overhead, and it lights Jake's face in a way that makes him look boyish. Like, thank god I paid Mischief so little attention way back when.

As I scan the drink menu, I pause at the description

of the Thyme & Thyme Again cocktail. I was planning on getting at least one, maybe two. But Jake won't be drinking, and I have no idea if my doing so might bother him or spoil any plans for after.

Angela has never minded hanging out while I've had a couple glasses of wine. But everyone is different, and it's sinking in that we barely know each other. I put the cocktail menu down. *I don't have to drink tonight*, I think. *It's not a big deal.*

Jake looks up. "Do you want to share? Try as much as possible?" He seems to notice that I've placed the drink list precariously at the edge of the table to prompt the waiter to take it. "And you should order a drink, if you want."

I try to play it cool, but as usual, my face is heating up, embarrassed by a question I haven't even asked.

"It's really fine," he says. "I know some people are prickly about it, but I've been sober for twelve years now. If I couldn't handle the sight of someone else drinking, I would have relapsed a really long time ago."

"No, I know. It just feels rude. And then I'll be buzzed."

Jake raises an eyebrow at me. "It's up to you," he says. "But if you want one, I'll enjoy watching you enjoy it."

Now my entire body is warm, and it's not from embarrassment. "OK," I say. "That works for me."

We're interrupted by our server coming over to take our orders. Jake grins up at him. "Hey, good to see you, Bryce." Bryce is clearly flustered—and pleased—to be recognized, but he regains his composure to get our beverage orders:

Gemma's rec for me, and a booze-free bitters and soda for Jake.

Once we're alone again, I ask, "Do you know everyone in town?"

Jake nods. "Pretty much. I mean, it is a small place. Plus, because of Gemma . . ." he shrugs. "I hear a lot about the inner workings of the Cabins."

He seems bashful, like he's trying to play it off or something. "I think it's really cool," I say. "That you have such a good community up here."

Jake looks pleased by this, like it genuinely hasn't occurred to him that he's on a first-name basis with people because he might be a part of something: a fixture in this place. "I guess so," he says.

"When you think about settling down, if that *is* something you want to do . . ." I want to be careful here. This situation is undeniably a date, but I wouldn't want him to take a question about his future the wrong way. I can't help my curiosity, though. "Would you ever do that here?"

Jake shakes his head. "I'm not really built for full-time small-town life," he says. "Or these winters."

"I don't know," I tease. "Think of all the skills you could pick up. Snowmobiling. Cross-country skiing. Ice fishing."

He laughs. "I've gone ice fishing," he says. "There's an ice hole at Lake Dunmore. Not my thing. Too much sitting around."

We put in our food order, and we talk about our adolescent jobs between bites of sourdough smeared with cultured butter—I worked at a camp in Michigan all through high school, and Jake spent one summer scooping ice cream at J. P. Licks before he began boy-banding. I give Jake the longer version of my transition from finance to flowers over charcoal-roasted lamb loin and miso-marinated cabbage. But the question I'd started to ask still lingers at the back of my palate the whole time.

After Bryce clears the dishes from our mains, I decide to go for it. We've drifted into a conversation about what does and doesn't constitute a midlife crisis, and I see my opening. "How did you end up traveling so much, anyway?" I ask.

He leans back in his chair, stretching his legs out under the table. One knee touches mine, and he lets it linger. I feel him pull away, and the sense of loss is much stronger than I expected.

"The first couple of years of sobriety really, really suck. I had to figure out how to be a person again in all these different ways. Whether to go to bars, and what to even do when I'm there. How to date. How to even—like, I wasn't sure how to tell jokes. If I could even be funny anymore."

He drains the last sips of his drink before continuing. "And being around people I knew—who knew the old me—made it feel ten times harder. Like my old self was a ghost, waiting for me around every corner. Around that time, I met a woman who was a travel influencer. She was going to Thailand, so I figured I'd go with her. Wasn't like I couldn't afford it." He shrugs, but I can tell that talking about this—wealth, the relative ease of his life—usually makes him uncomfortable. "It was such a relief to be in a place where no one knew me. Most people didn't even recognize me. I didn't speak the language. Actually, I've never talked about it this way before, but . . . I think I felt like an alien at home. And I felt like an alien in Thailand too, but at least there it made sense."

"And you've kept leaving ever since."

"I have."

Do you still feel like an alien? I wonder. *Do you feel like that with me?* Then I chastise myself: *Stop it, Maggie. Don't act like you're not like other girls. Like you're the person who can crack him.*

We pause to order an apple tart tatin to split, and I'm already wistful. As much as I'm looking forward to what—I hope—comes next, part of me is reluctant to leave the table. It's so easy sitting here with Jake, basking in the pleasure of his undivided attention, being continually surprised and delighted by the natural give-and-take of our chatter.

"I think I told you, my first day here, I felt so out of sorts. But whenever I'm hanging out with you I feel . . ." I have to search for a phrase that isn't *at home*, which is definitely way too intense, too soon. "Welcome," I finish.

Jake nods, but he's looking down, fiddling with the cuff of his shirt. I wonder if what I said was too much. To cover my potential faux pas, I lift my nearly empty highball glass in an attempt to pivot. "To the best vacation fling I've ever had," I offer.

He looks up; his eyes betray a touch of surprise, and then they settle. But he raises his glass, his gaze locked on mine, and echoes, "The best vacation fling."

XIV

JAKE

I'm glad she said that, I think. For a second there, I was starting to let myself feel dangerous things. But Maggie's toast was a good reminder of what the boundaries are. She said it herself: This is temporary. And that's best for the both of us.

"Jake," I hear Maggie say, with the tone of someone who is repeating herself. "Are you ready to go?"

The crumbs of our tart are all that's left on the plate, and I shake my head to snap myself out of my daze. Maggie's already standing and pulling her coat off the back of the chair. I do the same, and as we walk toward the exit, she reaches for my hand. "Want to come to mine?" she asks, her voice breathy. My heart seizes involuntarily. *It's just a fling.*

"Yeah. Yes," I say. "Let's get out of here."

We take the long way, meandering along the Cabins' paths, letting our stomachs settle. I wish I had brought a scarf or hat, but the cold does a good job forcing me back to reality. Not letting this get too intense is the smart thing to do, but it becomes harder to remember why when Maggie squeezes my hand and tilts her face up to look at the stars. "Is that Cassiopeia?" she whispers, her voice so reverent that I want to buy a telescope.

Maggie's cabin is around the far side of the lake, nestled in a copse of trees. The red car she drove to my house the other day is parked out front.

As she nudges the door open, I realize I haven't been in one of these in over a decade. They've redone them since then, and it's a relief that I don't recognize the interior. I don't want to overlay those miserable, booze-sick days onto tonight.

I shrug off my coat, taking in Maggie's belongings; some I recognize from the few days we've spent together: Her Shera Benoit book—nearly finished—sits on the coffee table, and the sweater she was wearing at the bar on that first night hangs over the back of a chair. There are no flowers in the room, and I wonder if that's been strange for her. Or if it really has been a relief to be away from her work.

Maggie drifts toward the small kitchen. "Do you want some water?" she offers.

"Sure." I follow her and watch her open a cabinet, pulling down two cups. I find myself wondering what her place in New York is like. How does she move through a space that is *actually* home?

Focus, Ramsey. You don't have that many of these moments left.

The thought makes me impatient. "Actually," I say,

"I think I'd rather have something else." I take the water glasses from her hands and set them gently on the counter beside her. She reaches for my sleeve, and I press my whole body into her, pushing us up against the kitchen wall.

Her nose finds the divot of my neck, and she inhales deeply, unabashedly. Her dress has a low back, and my hand clips under the fabric. Maggie shivers against me. "All dinner, I couldn't stop thinking about how badly I wanted to taste you again," I say.

Her breath gusts over my skin, and I have to swallow a moan. "You should, then."

At that, my knees threaten to buckle. I want to kneel in front of her, pull up her dress, and devour her out right here in the kitchen. I want to fuck her on the tiled floor, fast and desperate, like we're teenagers. But I don't know how many times I have left to do any of this, and I can't waste a single one. I make myself pull away slightly.

Maggie licks a line along the V of my open collar, then looks up at me, curls mussed, brown eyes glowing, lips already somehow bitten red. "And I've wanted to do that since I saw you at the hostess stand," she says. She's devastating when she's like this, surprised by her own boldness, and already leading me into the bedroom.

When she falls back onto the bed, I finally kiss her, and it's a relief. I gather the skirt of her dress in my hands, tugging it upward so that I can get to her skin underneath.

She's wearing tights—black and sheer but not sheer enough—and right now, I really hate them. "Take these off," I murmur against her neck.

We disentangle briefly so that she can scrub them down her legs. I'm about to step between her knees and start kissing her again when I notice something on her bedside table. It's in a small, discreet pouch; in theory, it could be anything. But I've been in enough women's bedrooms to have a good guess.

"Maggie," I say. "What's that?"

I thought I'd seen her blush before, but this is a new level. She goes scarlet, which I might mistake as sweet if she hadn't told me to go down on her only a few minutes ago. "My vibrator," she says.

I smirk. "Ah, right. Self-indulgence."

She shrugs, and there's a swagger to it, like she's already recovered from her brief embarrassment. "Well, I didn't expect you. And for better or worse, I like having plans."

I reach for the pouch. "Have you used it?" I ask.

She nods.

"Here?"

Nods again.

"Were you thinking of me?"

Maggie looks me right in the eye. "Yes."

The idea of her naked between these sheets, touching herself and picturing me, is enough to nearly undo me. I smile what I'm sure is a cocky smile, trying to envision it. But then I realize I don't have to.

"Show me," I say.

Maggie shakes her head. "But you're right here. I want you."

I place the vibrator down and turn back to her. "OK," I say. "But can I use it to touch you too?"

"Oh." Maggie's wide-eyed, like the possibility hadn't even occurred to her. "Yes."

I lean down to kiss her, maneuvering us both so that she's sprawled on the bed, bringing me down with her. Now when I pull her dress up, I get nothing but skin, and my dick twitches at the feel of her hot, wet center, already pulsing gently against my palm.

"Do you want to come fast," I ask. "Or slow?"

She bucks up into the pressure I'm giving her. "Hard to think when you're doing that."

"Take your time." I start to rub my thumb in slow, lazy circles against her clit.

"I want," she says, barely able to get the words out in this state. "I want you inside of me."

I bury my face in her neck. I'm dizzy with this woman, with her confidence, her openness. The way she's able to reel me in closer and closer by being herself, by being honest about her want and chasing it.

She pushes me back so that I'm kneeling between her thighs and then sits up and starts to unbutton my shirt. She's careful with it, and when she's done, she slides the fabric off my shoulders.

Then she pulls her own dress over her head.

She's braless, and her tits spill out, nipples already hard, begging to be kissed. I press her back onto the bed and focus on getting my mouth on as much of her as possible. I feel wild and reckless, but still laser-focused on how she's responding to me. On pulling more noises from her mouth, more wetness between her legs. I don't even realize that I'm rubbing my dick along the crease of her hip until she reaches down to unzip my pants and pulls it out.

"This time, I want to feel you while you come," she murmurs, running her thumb along the head.

"And I'm here to give you what you want."

Maggie pauses and meets my eyes. "What you want too," she says softly.

"Trust me," I tell her. "Fucking you is the only thing I want to do right now."

"Well." There's a smile in her voice as she wags a finger at my pants. "Take these off."

I didn't want to assume anything, but I did slip a condom into my back pocket before I left the house, and I find it as I step out of my pants and underwear and leave them puddled on the floor. When I slip the condom on and press the head of my cock against her core, I watch her eyes go wide.

She takes a deep breath. "More," she exhales.

I slide in a few inches and pause to give her a second to adjust. Her eyes flutter closed, and I wait until she tips her head back, exposing her throat, and directs me again: "More."

From there, it's almost too easy to sink deep inside her. To roll my hips against hers, matching each stroke to the hitches in her breathing. Maggie reaches back, bracing herself against the wooden bed frame, so that she can meet me thrust for thrust.

I almost get lost in the sheer, blissful sensation of us being so connected. Of the simple overwhelm of how fucking good this feels. But then my gaze lands on the bedside table. I reach over to grab the vibrator and press it into her hand.

"Can you show me?" I ask. "How did you do it when you were thinking about me?"

Maggie makes a strangled noise, something guttural and needy. She nods, presses the toy to life and places it against her clit, and we both look down at the space where our bodies meet. Her hips buck up helplessly when it starts to flutter against her.

"We'll do this again tonight," I assure her. And myself. "Then tomorrow morning," I say as we slowly start to find our rhythm again. "God, I would spend the rest of my life inside of you if I could. You feel so fucking good."

Maggie replies with a moan, squeezing her eyes tightly shut. Then the next thing I know, she's quivering underneath my hands, lightly cursing as she comes. I try to pull out a little, to let her better ride the wave, but she stops me, shaking her head as she pulses around my cock. "You sure?" I gasp. "I'm going to—"

"Fuck, Jake, that's what I want."

I come, pressing my chest against her tits and kissing her, open-mouthed and panting.

Then I face-plant into the sheets beside her, intending to steady myself and then get up. To clean myself off and head home. But Maggie wraps a knee around my thigh and tucks her head under my arm, and instead, I stay.

FRIDAY

XV

MAGGIE

In the morning, my body switches online before my brain does. For a few long moments, all I register is *warm* and *man* and *yes*. I mentally swim to the surface, passing through memories of last night: Jake's knee brushing mine under the table, our hands entwining as we left Basket. The way he held me against the wall in the kitchen and fucked me after. Coming with the vibrator, reminding us both how badly I wanted him before I had him.

By the time I'm fully conscious, I'm also wet, and I pull him toward me, unsubtly throwing a leg over his hip. He groans at the contact. "Maggie," he says, his voice still hoarse from sleep. "Oh my god."

It's obvious, but I ask anyway: "Do you want to?"

"Mmm." He smooths his hand over my hip and rolls toward me. Then his brain catches up. "I don't have any more condoms, though."

I'm almost tempted to say *fuck it*: I have an IUD, and it would feel so good to have him bare, this hard first thing in the morning. But my child-of-the-'90s sex education stops me.

Instead, I slowly slide down under the sheets, trailing my fingers down his chest and then his stomach, and take him in my mouth. His hips twitch at the initial shock of it, but as my throat opens up to him, his whole body goes pliant. His fingers tangle in my hair, and I tongue my approval.

After that, Jake convinces me to use the vibrator solo, and by the time we're ready for breakfast, it's midmorning. I call the lobby and have egg sandwiches delivered to the cabin so we can eat in our underwear, sprawled out on the corduroy couch in the living room. The sight of Jake in boxer briefs, padding around making coffee, is masturbation fodder I'll hold on to for years.

He's handing me my mug when his phone starts buzzing loudly in the other room. "Sorry, hang on. Only like five people have this number, so it could be important."

I take my first sip of the Americano, trying not to think too hard about the fact that I am now one of those five people who have Jake's number.

This place isn't big enough for me not to hear him say "Charlie!" as soon as he picks up. The rest of the call is muffled; it's mostly Jake making *I'm listening* noises and saying "Yeah, no" and "I agree."

There's a long stretch of quiet after he says goodbye. Long enough that I start to wonder if something's wrong, if he's grabbing his clothes from the bedroom and getting ready to leave. But when Jake emerges and joins me on the couch, he's still in his underwear.

"Everything OK?" I don't want to pry, but it feels stranger not to ask.

"Just Charlie calling to check in about something," he says. He squints a little, eyes crinkling like he's deciding whether to continue. "His wife, Maya, is a political consultant, and she's vetting the speakers for an event. One of them is an AA guy I know, so they wanted to see if I thought he'd be good."

"Will he be?"

Jake shrugs. "I think so." He reaches over to open the woven picnic basket containing our breakfast.

"If they need an AA guy, why didn't they just ask you?"

Jake's face is inscrutable when he replies, "They did." He pulls out the sandwiches and passes one to me. "But I can't do it. It's when I'll be in Berlin."

"Oh, right. You mentioned," I say. When he shared those plans, they felt completely irrelevant to my life. I'm surprised at the pang I feel remembering them, as if they're somehow more material to me now. When did I start imagining a hazy, gauzy future in which maybe somehow we both left Vermont at the same time and went back to New York and kept doing pretty much exactly this?

"I didn't want to do it anyway." Jake's tone is perhaps just a touch too forceful, like he's still trying to convince himself that it's true.

"Why not?" I ask.

"I hate public speaking. And yes, I know what I used to do for a living, but that wasn't about me. That was, like, a character I played. And anyway, people always think I'll have something really wise to say, instead of just, like, *Listen, I survived and I don't really know why*. And it'd be nice if I did. But I don't."

I nod slowly. Angela has to go to funerals every now and again—for women she met in rehab, or guys she used to drink with. It's the rare subject she never really talks about. "Not everyone makes it out alive," she said once. I will never forget it.

"What are you doing in Berlin?" I ask.

"Helping a friend set up an art exhibition," he says. "She's very particular, especially if it's new work."

"Sounds fun," I say. And it does, but part of me can't help thinking that it also sounds . . . kind of like another type of distraction. Like something he could potentially skip if a longtime friend and his wife asked him an important favor.

But what do I know about Jake's real life or his relationship with Charlie? And it's not fair to expect him to parade his trauma around so that random people can learn from it. He's well within his rights to say no, I remind myself.

We chat as we eat our way through breakfast about nothing of consequence. We drink a second cup of coffee. Eventually, Jake looks at his phone and frowns at the time. "I should probably go soon. Buster's people are going away for a few days, so they're bringing him over."

"Yeah," I say. "I mean, it is my last full day, so I should probably . . ." I don't know what I think I should probably do, except manage my own expectations.

"Yeah." Jake and I look at each other for a long moment. This could be goodbye.

"What if I came by tomorrow?" he asks, the words coming out in a jumble, like he's worried he won't be able to say them in time. "We could have breakfast or something, before you leave?"

Despite knowing this has to end at some point, whether that's today or tomorrow, I agree almost immediately.

Jake grins. He retrieves last night's clothes from the bedroom floor and leans over to press a long kiss to my forehead as he buttons his shirt.

XVI

MAGGIE

After he leaves, I take myself back to bed, mostly to escape the thoughts I don't have the energy to untangle. The thought that what Jake and I have is a genuine connection. The thought that I'm old enough, have experienced enough life, not to take that for granted. The thought that I came here to focus on myself and am instead obsessing over him.

No thank you. So I choose unconsciousness instead.

By the time I wake up, it's late afternoon, only a few hours of sunlight left. I force myself not to waste this day. I order in a late lunch and putter around the cabin for a bit, making gestures at starting to pack but letting myself get distracted by various nothings instead. For instance, I haven't made a single fire since I've been here, even though the pot-bellied woodstove is one of the selling points of this cabin. I get to work laying logs.

When my food arrives, I eat in front of the flames. My mind keeps replaying the conversation Jake and I had a few days ago about midlife crises. When I turned forty in

July, I barely had time to process it. It was during my busy season, and I was knee-deep in wedding bouquets. Plus, as I'd been told over and over by clients with personal trainers and med-spa appointments, forty is the new thirty. It didn't *feel* like a personal milestone, so I kept my eyes up and kept moving.

But now I wonder if some part of the recent cloud of malaise I've felt hovering over me has been the pressure of that number. A sense that I should have decided by now what the rest of my life will look likc. Instead, I'm plagued by open-ended questions: Will my business keep succeeding, or will it fail and force me to pivot—again? If it succeeds, will I keep wanting to do this forever? Have I figured it out yet, or will I just keep having to figure a new "it" out over and over and over again?

This thing with Jake has been all possibility, and I'm realizing that's what I've been missing: the excitement that comes with pursuing something simply because I want to, without worrying too much about potential future outcomes. Just because this little fling is about to end doesn't mean I can't take a lesson from it.

And it is about to end. I've known this all along, but now I let myself feel that fact. What Jake and I have is special, and rare, but it's also just as fragile as an exotic hothouse bloom. Made to flourish in specific conditions—and all too likely to perish outside of them.

At this point, the fire in the small stove is flagging, so I grab another log and toss it on. A small card next to the neat stack informs me that white birch was specifically chosen because of its sweet aroma, and that all the kindling is collected around the property.

I reach for one of the branches and turn it idly between my fingers, and a familiar part of my brain clicks on. I wonder how I might incorporate something like this into an arrangement. If it would be too rough or—

You still have a little more time before you have to think about work.

I put the branch down, expecting to feel released from some obligation. But instead of relief, I feel . . . disappointment.

So I pick it back up again, now a deliberate gesture. It's not that I have disliked my work recently, exactly. But for the last six months—maybe longer—it's just been feeling like nothing but *work.*

Holding this gnarled piece of snow-white wood doesn't feel that way. It feels tantalizing. Like possibility.

Maybe that's because there's no customer here. No expectations to meet, no color schemes to match. No off-limits flowers, no ideal arrangement heights. No invoices to fill out, no budgets to balance. There's just this little piece of tree between my fingers, waiting for me to see something more in it.

I rest it on the coffee table and head over to the bedroom, where all my clothes surround my suitcase, ready to be folded up and put away. I pull on my duck boots and a puffer jacket and—after a glance out the window reveals heavy gray skies—a beanie. My cabin doesn't have scissors, but I grab a steak knife from the kitchen and a stray plastic bag. I slip out into the afternoon drizzle to see what I can find.

As a kid at camp, I foraged, long before I knew that flowers could be sourced—and that *sourced* could be used as a verb like that. The woods that surround the Cabins are hardly in their fullest bloom, but as I wander the grounds, there's a surprising amount of foliage that catches my eye: Fallen sugar maple leaves that burst with color, wild blackberries that stain my fingertips purple. There are still a few stands of baby pink asters hanging on, and pale violet blooms of chicory too.

I fall back into a familiar rhythm: My desire manifests here, too, as I remember what it feels like to see something and really want it. To experience its pull. I bend down in the damp dirt and separate out stems and twigs and blossoms as carefully as I can.

As the sun disappears, the cold starts seeping through my clothes. I know it's time to head back to the cabin. Once inside, I shed my wet layers, pull on dry, warm sweats, and immediately get to work sorting and arranging my bounty in a plain, tall water glass. I don't allow myself to think too hard about what I'm doing; my brain is quiet for once, my eyes and hands guiding me as I shuffle each find into pleasing shapes and patterns.

When it feels finished, I step back to take it in. The birch juts up on the left, and a spray of blackberries cascades down the right side. Aster and chicory mingle with the maple leaves like they might still be on the forest floor. It's nothing I would create for a client. It wouldn't even really work in my apartment. It's wild and strange. It feels like the week I've just spent here, actually: unplanned and unexpected. A little messy. It looks like something only I could make, but only when I wasn't getting in my own way.

SATURDAY

XVII

JAKE

On Maggie's last morning in St. John's Cross, we meet up at the hotel's lobby restaurant for breakfast. She gets there before me, and for a second, it's like the first night, and we're strangers again. When I catch a glimpse of her leaning against the bar, it immediately sends me back to Sunday. The same curl falls over her forehead, but now I know that's just what it does.

I don't think I've stopped thinking about her for a second since we parted ways yesterday. It felt nearly impossible to tear myself from her cabin, especially with the promise of a real goodbye looming. So at some point last night, alone and tangled in my sheets, wide-eyed and sleepless, I made a reckless decision: I'm going to tell her I want to keep seeing each other.

Our chemistry is undeniable, but Maggie's given me no reason to believe she sees me as anything more than a several-night stand, a guy she met—and fucked—on vacation. But as I kept turning the idea over in my mind, every way I looked at it, it felt more painful not to try than to face rejection. At least I would know exactly where I stood instead of wondering *what if.*

That conversation is nagging like a pebble in my shoe as I walk over to her. I'm so distracted mentally composing what I'm going to say—and when I'm going to say it—that it takes me a second to notice exactly who she's talking to. In another bit of symmetry to our first night, it's the Cabins' reliably smarmy concierge, Eric.

"Ramsey!" he crows. I shake off the oncoming cringe. "Good to see you. I can't believe I missed your first time at Basket the other night—I had to hear about it from Bryce. You really should have let us know you were coming. We would have given you the full VIP experience."

"No need," I say. It must come out a bit gruff, because Maggie's smile turns up a notch like she sees how I'm handling my annoyance.

"Well, I'm here this morning," Eric says, clasping his hands at his waist. "So we'll send out some new additions to the breakfast menu for you to try."

I feel like someone has lowered the oxygen in the room by 10 percent. I can still breathe, but it's harder, a shift in altitude. Being given special treatment always makes me feel trapped. It reminds me of being eighteen or nineteen and shuttled around to these dinners hosted by our record label: endless nights gladhanding strangers, making forced small talk. It reminds me of being purposefully seated in the center of a restaurant, left to wonder whose eyes were on me. Worrying who might be listening in on my conversations, looking for a tip they could sell to a tabloid. It tugs on some old instinct. Makes my hackles go up.

I have no idea how anyone survives being that famous now. At least people didn't have smartphones with cameras back then.

I've spent the morning trying to get to a calm and level-headed place—woke up early, went for a run—but that all flies out the window as Eric escorts us to a table. Normally, breakfast orders at the Cabins are taken coffee shop–style at the counter, but he's making a show of it. Naturally the other diners notice.

After Eric insists on taking our drink orders himself, he finally leaves us, and it's just me and Maggie. She leans an elbow on the table and rests her chin in her palm, giving me a good look, as if it's been longer than twenty-four hours since she last saw me. I wonder if she's feeling as enthralled with me as I am with her. "Hi," she says.

She brings her fingers to the little vase of wildflowers between us, and I realize that I haven't touched her since I got here. The table makes it awkward, but I softly nudge her foot with mine. "Hi," I say back. I take a deep breath. It's easy to relax when I can just focus on Maggie. This woman. These possibilities. "How was the rest of your day yesterday?"

A smile spreads over her face. "It was really good, actually. This trip—I kind of can't believe how well it worked. I'm actually looking forward to going back to the city and starting work on Monday. Is that crazy?"

"It is crazy," I say with a hint of teasing.

"And what about you?" she asks. "Did you pack for Berlin?"

"Not quite yet. Most of what I'm bringing is actually in the city." *OK. Here's my opening.* "And I was thinking—"

We're interrupted by Eric dropping off our coffees, plus a pair of financiers on a small plate. "On the house, for my VIPs," he says. That's the second time he's called me a VIP today, and it makes my skin crawl. The idea that I'm somehow "very important" and everyone else here is just a pleb. Merely scenery for my washed-up stardom.

Eric lingers while Maggie bites into the pastry and makes an appreciative noise. He leans in closer, like he needs her to say something, and it's absolute torture.

She inches her chair forward, and Eric finally gets a clue. He bows at the waist, and I feel my eyes narrow as he backs away.

"Sorry, you were saying something earlier?" Maggie asks me. "About—"

"Excuse me," someone interrupts. I look up to see a woman standing next to the table, an eager light in her eyes. Now my heart really sinks. I know exactly what that looks means; it's a look I've been given thousands of times. It means she's about to say—*Yep, here she goes.* "I feel terrible about intruding on your breakfast. But I would never forgive myself if I didn't say something. I was—*I am*—the hugest Mischief fan."

Luckily, the appropriate response to this has been drilled into my body for decades now. "Wow," I say, giving an

Oscar-worthy performance of a well-mannered celebrity. "Thank you so much. What's your name?"

It's Jen. Mischief at Fenway Park was her first concert, and from the way she asks after Charlie, I can tell he was her favorite. I used to get offended at those sorts of things, but not anymore. We take a quick selfie, and I catch a few other people snapping pictures of us as we do so. All while Maggie silently watches. I wonder what she makes of the spectacle of my everyday life.

The worst part is that I can't blame any of them. Not Jen for saying hi and telling me about how Mischief's music changed her life, and not everyone else who's done the same in the past or will do so in the future. I can't even blame the lookie-loos who think they're slyly capturing the moment from afar—people who figure as long as we're taking a picture, they're OK to take one too. If I'm being my most gracious self, I can't even blame Eric, who is just doing what he thinks is his job. (But I will blame Eric. Fuck that guy.)

But today the pressure of it all feels extra oppressive, crowding against me, nudging me into a corner I can't escape. Maybe it's because St. John's Cross is usually my hideaway, where I can avoid a scene like this. I feel like I'm looking down a long tunnel at two versions of myself: One is the private person, Jake, who's working up the courage to be my most vulnerable self with Maggie. The other is the public persona of Ramsey, trying to manage the affections of strangers to make sure that he's not letting anyone down.

I tried to describe this split consciousness to a therapist

once. "Who's doing the looking, then?" she'd asked. I didn't know how to answer her.

"Sorry about that," I say to Maggie once Jen has gone back to her breakfast.

"How often do you get that?" Maggie asks.

I shrug. "Comes and goes, honestly. But the problem is, once someone breaks the seal—" I can already see another woman getting up to approach us. *She's trying to be nice*, I remind myself. *This is a special moment for her.*

But the thing is, this was supposed to be *my* special moment. My time with Maggie. Maybe the last time we'll have together. An angry, hurt part of me wonders if Eric did this on purpose: draw attention to my presence here in order to make sure that there would be pictures of me at the Cabins posted online. He could never do that himself, but if guests happen to take photos and share them and tag the hotel, well . . .

"I'm sorry," I say to the second woman, before she's even had a chance to ask. "I can't take any more pictures right now."

"It's just that my sister is—" she says.

"I'm having breakfast," I say. "With a friend."

The woman turns automatically to Maggie. "Sorry," she says directly to her. Then she stands there like she's waiting for Maggie to say something. Introduce herself, maybe.

I'm much more mature than I used to be: kinder, less impulsive. But the worst version of me still lives somewhere deep inside, a bundle of nerves waiting to fire. It takes every ounce of self-restraint I possess not to snap, *Don't talk to her!*

I have to leave this room. "Sorry," I say to them both. Then, just to Maggie: "I'm just gonna go outside for a minute. I need some air."

If people weren't looking at me before, they're certainly watching me make my way across the restaurant and out the lobby doors. For a long moment I just stand there, sucking in cold air, reminding myself that I'm not actually trapped. I'm OK.

I'm OK.

I hear the doors swinging open behind me and catch the sound of Maggie's gait as she comes to stand next to me. "You all right with company?" she asks.

"Yeah."

"OK."

We stand side by side in silence. I try to be in my body. I blow warm air on my hands. All my mental preparation—the thoughtful, adult conversation I was going to have with her—it's all gone out the window now. I quit smoking last year, but *god* do I want a cigarette right now.

"I'm sorry," Maggie says, and I sense her eyes on my face.

"For what?"

"I guess I'm sorry that that happened at all."

I turn toward her. She's luminous in the morning light: the soft pink curve of her cheeks and the warm, rich brown of her eyes.

"I'm sorry too," I say. "I was—I had a plan for how this was going to go."

"Oh yeah?"

"Yes," I say. I rest my gaze on her face, wishing I didn't

see concern there. "What I was trying to say back there was that I'm going to be in New York for a few days before Berlin. And so I was going to ask if we could see each other. Again. In the city." There. Whatever else happens, I did it. It's done.

Maggie looks surprised, then happy, and for a moment I think she's going to kiss me. But then something appears to occur to her, and her smile fades. She looks at me carefully. "Jake," she says.

At the way she says my name, my heart cracks in half, but she continues like she has to get her words out. "I've loved these days with you. Better than anything I could have imagined, honestly. But I'm not . . ." She sighs and pushes her hair off her face in a frustrated gesture. "I'm afraid it's not going to work long-term."

I shake my head. "How are you going to find out if we don't try? Maggie—" But I'm interrupted by a couple coming out of the hotel's doors. Of course: It's checkout o'clock. I put a hand on her shoulder, and she lets me guide her around the side of the building, where we have some privacy.

There, she leans against the wooden wall and looks up at me, a frown furrowing her brow. "What do you mean," she says, "by try?"

"What do you mean, what do I mean? I drive back to the city in a couple of days and take you out to dinner. Maybe drinks, or coffee, or I don't know. We hang out. Talk. We—" I take a step toward her, closing the gap between us, but the look on her face stops me from reaching out to touch her.

"And then," she says, "you go to Berlin."

"Well, yeah, but then I come back."

I've seen that look on women's faces before. She's about to let me down gently. I hate that she feels like she has to be gentle with me.

"Jake, the person you've been hanging out with this week—that was Vacation Maggie. She's me taking a break from my life and trying to fight off burnout. My real life is client demands and delivery schedules and shipment delays and Valentine's Day offers. Yours is going to New York for a few days, and then Berlin, and then somewhere else. Your life is . . ."

Vacation is what she's thinking. But she doesn't have the heart to say that.

It's a devastating diagnosis. "I—I don't have plans after Berlin" is all I come up with as a response.

"It's not that I don't want to see you," Maggie says. "It's that this has been so perfect. And I just—I want to keep it that way. A little bubble of possibility. Of a week when I got every single thing I wanted. But that's not something that happens in the real world. It just . . . isn't."

I want to argue with her, but my self-loathing catches in my throat. Ever since Charlie and Maya's wedding, I've been caught between two worlds. There's the way I've been living, untethered and rootless. I can feel that I've outgrown it. But what comes next is a complete unknown. I want Maggie. But can I really change my life enough to keep her? What if I do, and it wrecks me? What if I don't, and it wrecks both of us? That might be worse than just letting her go.

My silence must say what I can't, because Maggie reaches out a hand and puts it on my wrist. Her fingers are cold. "Thank you for everything," she says. "This has been—" She pauses. "Well, I'll never forget it." She rises up on her tiptoes to press a kiss to my cheek. And then she walks away.

BACK IN THE CITY

XVIII

MAGGIE

When I head to Montague Diner for breakfast a few days after I get home, I'm in a mood. It's a Thursday with the kind of crappy, drizzly weather that makes it known that fall is quickly giving way to winter, a season I hate both personally and professionally. I try to work with local product when it's possible, but this time of year—and my increasingly picky and demanding clientele—means that for the next four or five months, most of the flowers I use will have been shipped from warmer climates. I'm resentful of pretty much everything until I slide into a booth and look up at Ang grinning conspiratorially at me.

Angela's take on sobriety is embracing the joy she's found through it. As far as she's concerned, she should have died several times in her twenties, which means that now, even a nasty New York morning is an unexpected gift. I try to let some of that positivity rub off on me as I catch the waitress's eye to order a coffee.

"OK, we're skipping small talk," she announces. "And

don't you dare ask me about myself. I'm fine. It's been a week here, nothing's changed. I need every single detail about your *whirlwind rockstar vacation thing*, stat."

"He was more of a pop star."

Angela laughs, shooing my correction away with her hands like it's a fly. "The closest I've ever gotten was my high school boyfriend whose band headlined punk nights at the local rec center. So as far as I'm concerned, this counts."

Our waitress returns with my coffee, and I wrap both hands around the mug, greedily absorbing its warmth. The last time I really talked to Angela was a follow-up to my stoned texts at the Cabins. I told her that I had slept with Jake and that she was going to hear the rest of the story in person. So she has no idea what to expect.

Neither do I, really. When I think about Jake from a few days' distance, I get the same stomachachey twist of desire I did when I was with him. Now it's just accompanied by a lingering, miserable ache. It's like a splinter that has no right to be as painful and distracting as it is: such a seemingly small thing becoming somehow excruciating. I was so proud of myself when I walked away back in Vermont. It seemed like the adult thing to do: to recognize our affair for what it was—and what it wasn't.

But since then, my resolve has only weakened, and doubt keeps creeping further and further in.

But here with Angela, I have to start at the beginning. So I tell her about the fun parts: Spotting him at the bar and the thrill of running into him again at Perry Hill. The charge of every moment leading up to our first kiss; how I felt like an electrical storm, sparking static into the air, looking for somewhere to land.

"Hold on," Angela interrupts my flow. "You actually said, 'Thank you for indulging me'?"

"I cannot describe to you how feral I was at that point, Ang." By now, I'm well-caffeinated and midway through my plate of corned beef hash, and I'm much more animated than I was half an hour ago. "I had just come my fucking brains out; the mind-to-mouth filter was not functioning."

But as I consider what to share next, my mind leaps to my last conversation with Jake, and I can feel a shadow passing across my face. I don't hide it in time, and Angela leans forward instantly. "Oh no," she says. "Did he make it weird after? Say something, or . . . ?"

"No," I cut in before she can spin up a crime for Jake to have committed. "He didn't make it weird. It just . . ."

Angela knows me well enough that my pause makes her suspicious. "I mean, not to jump ahead—you *will* be filling in the details—but are you gonna see him again?"

"He's not—no. We're not going to see each other again."

Angela narrows her eyes thoughtfully. "Your decision? His?"

I shrug.

"I see." I thought I didn't want to talk about this part, but now I find myself eager to explain. To get Angela to tell me I did the right thing. So I skip straight to our last interaction. How it felt to watch him flee the restaurant.

How it reminded me that he was leaving the country in a matter of days. This image I have of him bouncing from one place to another, never taking anywhere or anyone—himself included—too seriously. How it all kind of broke my heart.

"Well, this sucks," Angela says succinctly.

I nod. "It does."

"I'm sorry that he didn't want to continue this in New York, but—" When I grimace, she cuts herself short. "What?"

"Well, he kind of did."

"But you didn't? OK, Mags, I think I'm missing something here. Why the fuck not?"

"I'm forty, Ang. He's not ready for an actual adult relationship with a forty-year-old."

"He said that?"

Angela's phone is sitting on the table, and I can see it starting to blink with incoming messages. We both have to get to work soon.

I sigh, pushing my plate to the side. "It's just . . . it's obvious, OK?"

She gives me a look like there's a lot more she wants to say, but maybe now isn't the time. I put on my best impression of a smile. "And anyway, it was a great vacation. I didn't work. Except on the last day when I made a completely unhinged arrangement." I scroll through my photos and pass her my phone.

"I think the phrasing is: unhinged, complimentary." She raises her brows.

I laugh. "Yeah, well, it felt good, but it's not like I could make anything like this for the Barbara Randolphs of the world."

"Well then, Margaret Lewis." She searches the diner to ask for our check. "I guess it's a good thing you didn't start your business for Barbara Randolph."

XIX

JAKE

I spend the week after Maggie leaves working on the bookcase. I started the project in June, and if I'm really being honest with myself, I don't think I ever planned on finishing it. I've liked having it to tinker with; I've liked fantasizing about what the finished product could be if I did everything right, knowing that's an impossibility.

But now, in the last days of October, I work like a man possessed. I fit each piece together with an almost maniacal precision; I spend hours making sure that it will sit perfectly flush against the wall. I keep my hands busy to avoid a spiral of self-destruction. So that I can think about something other than the feeling of Maggie's final kiss on my cheek, her icy fingers on my wrist. Her doubts about me feeding my own, an endless, toxic feedback loop.

I'm well aware that I'm distracting myself so that I don't have to deal with the real problem at hand. But it feels completely impossible to do anything else but keep myself moving.

I work so methodically that when I realize I'm done, it feels like an accident. For two days I've been steadily checking items off a to-do list without ever quite understanding that the list would eventually run out. But it finally does, it's four p.m., and the sun has almost set. I find myself standing in front of a beautiful, empty bookcase, my hands empty too. And I hear myself think, quite clearly, *This would be a perfect time for a drink.*

I have enough practice to stop that train of thought on its tracks. There's no alcohol in the house, and I'm sure as shit not about to get in the car to buy some. But I'm unnerved by how seamlessly it happened. How easy it felt, all of a sudden, that I might have just reached out and grabbed a drink. If it had been there.

I grab my phone and text Gemma, *accountability: I'm going to Burlington tomorrow.* There's a nine a.m. meeting in a bookstore's back room that's my fail-safe. It's the place I go when Gemma's and my informal checkup chats aren't strong enough.

I have a complicated relationship with AA proper. For a long time, I rejected it for being both cultish and corny. But traveling as much as I do, I need something solid in my life, a routine that can pull me out of spirals on dark days. And in every city I've ever been in, I can always find a group of fuckups in a basement somewhere, drinking cheap coffee and quoting The Big Book. It's saved me more times than I'd like to admit.

She writes back a few minutes later, *I'll come with.*

Gemma lets me get away with a silent forty-five-minute drive to Burlington, probably because she's not a morning person. We're both enough of regulars here that we get head nods when we walk through the doors. Randy, a seventy-something with a thick gray beard, always makes a point of giving me a hug, a handshake, and a hearty "welcome back" when he thinks I've been away for too long, and he does it today.

Then we take our places on folding chairs and wait for the ritual to begin. I didn't grow up religious, so this is the closest thing to church I know. The greetings, the reading, the speaker taking her place at the podium. There's even a call-and-response.

Today the whole thing brings me back to the earliest days of my sobriety. To the days I got during stints that didn't stick. How many times I've sat down and tried to believe that my life wasn't too broken to fix. It reminds me of a quote I once heard in a yoga class: "You're never too old, never too bad, never too late, and never too sick to start from scratch once again." *Never too bad, never too late.* The *never too bad* hits harder today.

When we're done, Gemma asks if I want to get coffee—real, drinkable coffee—and take a walk along the lakefront path. There's a cold wind blowing in off the water, but it's almost nice, the way it stings my skin, like a constant reminder I'm alive.

"So," she says. "What's up?"

"I had a moment last night," I tell her. "A scary one. Just needed a reset."

"It seems like you've been having a lot of moments lately."

I glance over at Gemma. She's wearing a cherry-red beanie with a Two Peas Farm patch, and she's looking straight ahead, like she doesn't have an agenda. She's just stating a fact. It's not like she's wrong.

And last night spooked me enough that I want to talk. "It's been kind of a time."

She doesn't give me shit for how long it has taken me to share this with her. "Want to tell me about it?"

I tell her about Maya and Charlie's wedding, and how it made me feel lonely in my own relationship. How I broke up with Kelsey and drove north to hole up in peace. And how into that peace came Maggie, the embodiment of everything I'd been wanting and was too scared to go after: someone who was so sure of pursuing her own wants that it made me feel like it was time to stop concealing mine.

"But she was right," I say as we turn to head back toward the car. The cold has gone from bracing to sharp since we've been out, and I'm ready to be warm again. "I do just go from place to place to avoid making any real decisions about what I want my life to be. But also, it would be crazy to change my whole life for someone I spent a week with."

"I mean, it would be crazy if it was just for her," Gemma says. "But it kind of sounds like that's what you want to do anyway."

I shrug. "I've been wrong about what I wanted. Lots of times. Or at least what was good for me."

"I guess." Gemma pauses to toss her empty coffee cup into a trash can. "But Jake, can I be . . . honest for a second?"

"I thought you were always honest."

Gemma rolls her eyes. "I don't lie to you, obviously," she says. "But I don't always say everything I'm thinking. And it sounds like I've been thinking the same thing you have. That you've outgrown your current, uh, lifestyle. That it's time to try something new. Regardless of whether it works out with Maggie or not."

"Yeah, but . . ."

"But what?"

"What if I screw it up?"

"You think that staying in one city for six months is going to be harder than getting sober was?" Gemma asks. "Than staying sober *is*?"

I clench my hands in my pockets. I don't know how to explain to her that I do think it will be. "That was just stopping," I say eventually. "Not doing something. This is . . ."

Wanting. Trying. Sticking around, opening up, being available. Not always keeping my eyes on the exit, waiting for the other shoe to drop.

Gemma seems to get what I mean. "Yeah," she says. We've reached her car, and we slip inside quickly. She turns the key halfway in the ignition so that the heat clicks on, coming to life with a roar. "I guess the question is: Would you rather try or stay stuck? Because from the outside, your life looks all freewheeling or whatever, but I see how trapped you feel."

When she puts it that way, it sounds so obvious: that this coping mechanism isn't serving me or the people I love. One of the things about getting sober is that, all of a sudden, when I look back on the years of my life—the ones I remember, anyway—I see so much pain. The pain I was in; the pain I was causing. Realistically, I know I'll never make it up to everyone I betrayed or let down or just disappointed from afar. And so, for a long time, I've found increasingly creative ways to keep people from getting too close to me. Even Gemma I only see three months out of the year.

"You're a grown-up, Jake," Gemma says, turning the key the rest of the way, letting the engine catch. "Your life is only going to change if you change it."

XX

JAKE

A few days later, I leave St. John's Cross and head south. It snowed yesterday but didn't stick, and the roads are thankfully clear. I wait until I'm on the interstate to call Charlie and make plans to have dinner with him and Maya this week.

Then I bite the bullet and call Katia to tell her I'm not coming to Berlin. She's disappointed but sounds more curious than anything. "This project is wood and wool, bunch of your hobbies combined," she laughs. "What happened? You have other plans?"

"Not yet," I tell her. "But I'm trying to make some."

I show up at Charlie and Maya's a few days later with a jug of Vermont maple syrup in hand. I couldn't bring myself to consider flowers without getting them from Maggie, and that didn't feel like the next right move, if I decide there is a next move.

When. I'm trying to think like that now. *When I decide.*

Charlie ushers me inside with his usual warmth. He's still got a bit of a tan going from their Maldives honeymoon; he looks good. Relaxed. Maya's finishing up some calls, so I drink a seltzer while I watch Charlie put the finishing touches on roasted chicken thighs. He tells me more about their trip and the work he's starting to do on a potential new album.

"And what about you?" he asks as we start pulling down plates to set the table. "How was your northern retreat this time?"

"Good," I say. "I needed it. It gave me time to do some thinking. And actually—well, I want to wait until Maya's here to tell you both."

"Tell me what?" Maya asks. She's just emerged from her office, looking somehow casual and glamorous, as usual. She gives me a quick kiss on the cheek, and then a longer one to Charlie. She's been drinking tea; Charlie has the kettle ready for her to pour herself a refill before she perches herself on a counter stool. "Now, Ramsey. What's going on?"

"I just canceled my trip to Berlin. I canceled all my trips, actually. I'm thinking I'm gonna try to be here more." After talking to Gemma, I decided that this was the first step. To literally stop running. See if I can slow down and handle my own life for a while.

Then maybe see if Maggie will let me back into hers.

"I like to hear that," Maya says, grabbing silverware to bring into the dining room. "It'll be nice to have you around more. Especially because . . ." She looks at Charlie. "You want to tell him?"

"I thought we weren't telling people yet."

I'm looking back and forth between their faces. Are they really about to—

"I'm already tired of keeping it a secret," Maya says. "And since we're all sharing news."

"Well." Charlie turns to me, the biggest, stupidest smile on his face. "We're pregnant."

"*I'm* pregnant, how dare you," Maya says.

"I didn't know how to say it! I haven't had practice," Charlie laughs as I launch myself at him, hugging him too hard. I've always thought that he'd make an incredible dad if he decided to be one, but he's always said he was ambivalent about fatherhood. Then he met Maya.

"Oh my god," I say, and I think I might be crying, just a little bit. "Oh my god, congratulations!"

Charlie is squeezing me tight, his face buried in my shoulder. "You're the first person we've told, aside from our families."

"I'm honored," I tell him. I'm also incredulous that we could possibly be having this conversation. It feels like yesterday that we were kids together, and then we were suddenly kids who were famous together. Now we get to be adults together, and that's an experience I want to have with Charlie too. I want to throw myself into the role of Uncle Ramsey. And unlike with Devin's daughter, who was born when I was too fucked up to take it seriously, I'll really be around. Maybe this time, I'll be Uncle Jake.

We spend the rest of dinner talking about the pregnancy: Maya's morning sickness that somehow arrives at the stroke of midnight. Whether they're going to move before the baby comes and how they haven't even started talking about names yet.

After, Charlie and I sit in the living room, drinking tea, and he decides it's back to my life. "So what changed your mind, anyway? Made you decide you wanted to drop your nomadic lifestyle and hang out with us normies in New York?"

"Says the guy who toured in Europe for a month last year," I tease him. "No, but—I met someone." Charlie's face immediately lights up, and I have to interject, "I'm not sure if we have a future. But she made me want to try to do things differently. I guess I'd been wanting to already. But she made me think it was time to, you know. Actually get started."

"I'm glad. I really want that for you, Ramsey."

It means more than I want to admit to hear Charlie say that. To know that even after everything we've been through, and everything I've put him through, he still sees possibility in me.

Maya comes in with a bar of dark chocolate, which she breaks into pieces, one for each of us. Then she settles on the couch next to Charlie, tucking her feet under his thighs.

"Now that I'm going to be in town, I'd really like to come to the fundraiser," I tell her.

"Well." Maya raises an eyebrow. "I swear I wasn't going to push, but we actually haven't secured the right speaker yet. I figured Elena could just do the in-conversation, but I really think it would be more meaningful if we had someone else who's, you know. Been through it."

The idea brings me up short, and my instinct is to balk.

Refuse responsibility. But I can't help but ask, "Are you sure you want me? I mean, Charlie knows—I'm not much of a public speaker."

"I'd prep you," Maya says. "But if you don't want to do it, I get it."

Another thing I'm trying to do is to sit still with my feelings of discomfort when they come on like this. To try to understand *why* I don't want to deal with something, instead of just ignoring it. "Can I think about it?" I ask.

"Of course. Also, that reminds me, Charlie—"

I tune out for a second while Maya and Charlie chat idly about the event. *Why don't I want to do this?* I ask myself. In part, it's just my usual allergy to being the center of attention. The way all spotlights feel poison-edged to me at this point.

But it's more than that. It's the stuff I was saying to Maggie in Vermont about not being sure why I got so lucky to survive it all. It's the conversation I had with Gemma about being afraid that I'm still screwing everything up. It's that twelve years ago I was able to make the decision to stay alive, but I've never really figured out how to allow myself to establish who I am in all the life that's left to me.

But I'm not doing that anymore. I'm not living scared. So fuck it. Before I leave, I tell Maya that I'm in.

Maya wasn't kidding about making sure I was properly prepared. She has me come over three times over the course of the next week to talk about my experiences and make sure I know Elena's accomplishments and policy proposals. She gets me to say things I never thought I'd admit out loud, and sometimes I'm even almost comfortable saying them.

After each session, I can't stop thinking about Maggie. All the things I told her and all the things I didn't get the chance to. The conversations I want us to have. It's like now that I've started talking, I don't want to stop. I keep thinking I'll run into her. Now that I'm claiming this city of eight million people, it feels like something that could happen.

I had planned to wait longer. To be sure that, by the time I called her, I was exactly who I wanted to be.

But with all this talking, I'm realizing that process will likely take the rest of my life. Into another lifetime, even. And I miss her. I want her to be part of this. To watch me changing, if she wants to. I want to change along with her.

So I get the go-ahead from Maya to extend her an invite. Three days before the event, I send Maggie a text: *I know how we left things, so ignore this if nothing's changed for you. But I've been thinking a lot about what I want from my life, and how to get it. I decided not to go to Berlin and will be in New York for the foreseeable future. And I'm speaking at the fundraiser I told you about. It would mean a lot to me if you were there to witness it. No expectations, though.*

XXI

MAGGIE

The morning of the fundraiser, I'm not sure if I'm going to go. As I work on my orders for the day, I try not to think about the event or about Jake in general. Instead, I keep turning over what Angela said to me at the diner: That I didn't start my business for Barbara Randolph. That I started it for myself. I literally called the business Margaret, but even though my name is on it, there is very little evidence of my hand—anything essentially Maggie—in it right now.

When I quit Goldman, I was excited, energized by the potential. Sure, fear was lurking in the background, but I let my desire to make this change, and to do it my way, tug me forward into the unknown.

And then, at some point, fear got back into the driver's seat. There was safety in putting my head down and doing the work and meeting other people's wants and needs. Or at least it felt like there was.

As I picture the arrangement I made the last evening at the Cabins, I put aside the tidy bouquet in front of me. And I let my hands tell me what they want. Instead of reaching for pearly white Ecuadorian roses, I trim Montauk daisies short and reach for eucalyptus branches, leaving them tall and untamed. I think of Jake and his projects—his carpentry, his knitting—and the creative flow he finds just simply making something. I add a few of my favorite ranunculus, bursting open so joyously they look overripe, and asters the same shade of pink I'd found in Vermont.

It won't work for the delivery that needs to be made this afternoon. But I have a feeling I know exactly where it belongs.

When I show up at the Upper East Side apartment building for the fundraiser, my name is on the doorman's list, and he escorts me to the main elevator instead of through some side entrance.

The doors slide shut, and I'm confronted with my own reflection in their mirrored finish. My cheeks are pink from the cold outside; the stray grays in my hair catch and reflect the fluorescent lights overhead. Here I am, I think. I'm hit all over again by the reality that I'm forty and I have nothing figured out, and I might never have anything all the way figured out, actually. And still, I'm doing this. I'm really, actually doing it.

At first I wrote off how much I missed Jake. Told myself it was evidence that I needed to get laid more often, a natural reflex after such an excellent week of sex and conversation. But over the last three weeks, that ache has only deepened, to the point where it's become impossible to ignore. When I walked away, I thought I was taking the mature, adult path by shutting him down at the end of my vacation. Instead, I was making the mistake I've made before—and will probably make again—of conflating being a grown-up with doing what I think grown-ups should do instead of doing what I, a grown-up who can make her own choices, want.

But now that I'm just minutes away from seeing him again, my heart thumps heavily in my chest; it's like I feel my blood everywhere, running wild with hope and want once again. God, what we had in St. John's Cross was so good. And if it could be what I think it could be—

The elevator chimes, and the doors slide open.

I step into a foyer where someone takes my coat and hands me a glass of champagne. I'm not sure I can handle a drink right now, but I'm grateful to have something to do with my hands. I'm trying to find the least conspicuous corner where I can hide out when I hear a woman say my name. "Maggie?"

I turn around to find myself face-to-face with Maya McPherson. She's exactly as beautiful as she is in pictures, but taller than I expected. She makes her pale-gray suit look so stylish that I suddenly wish I'd worn pants instead of a deep-green silk dress. "Ramsey said to keep an eye out for you. Hi," she says, reaching out to shake my hand. "I'm Maya."

"Maggie. Is he—?"

"He and Charlie are doing their old warm-up routine in

one of the bedrooms," she says. "Vocal exercises, the whole bit. I think it's mostly Charlie's attempt to keep him out of his head."

"Not an easy job."

She grins at me. "So you *do* know him."

"I hope so."

Maya holds up a finger to someone across the room and gives them a nod. "OK, I need to circle up with my candidate," she says to me. "Grab a seat anywhere, and hopefully I'll see you after?"

I'm settling into an oversize armchair tucked into a corner as Maya goes up to the mic stand at the front of the room to greet everyone. She tees up her candidate, Elena, who begins a short preamble, introducing Jake and his conversation partner, Jerome. He looks like he's in his late forties, a Black man with gray stubble on his chin and soft, kind eyes.

I barely process a word of the preamble. Because there is Jake, standing at the entrance to the living room, waiting to take the stage. His smile lines are still there around his mouth and eyes, but other parts of him have been smoothed, like he's been buffed into a big-city version of himself. His button-down is definitely designer, and polished leather boots have replaced his mud-splattered shitkickers. My mouth still waters at the sight of him.

He's focusing on Maya and Elena, but as he walks to take his seat facing the audience, he glances out over the crowd. When his gaze finds mine, we share a smile. Whatever happens after this, I know I'll be glad I came.

I'm proud he's doing this and grateful that I'm here to experience it.

The conversation starts with Jerome telling the short version of his story. He's a New York native, he explains, grew up in Washington Heights and went to Bronx Science for high school. But when he was a teenager, he was the victim of a hit-and-run car accident that left him with chronic pain—and a prescription that quickly turned into an opiate addiction. He's now been clean for five years and works as a counselor at the rehab facility where he got sober.

Jake nods when he's finished. "Thank you for sharing that, and congratulations on five years. That's huge. Something to celebrate. But I wanted to ask: When was the first time you *wanted* to get sober?"

Jerome nods thoughtfully. "A long time before that. Probably the first time I went to a pill mill for a scrip. That's a doctor who exists mostly to write prescriptions for people like me, people who need more than a regular doctor is willing to prescribe." He shifts slightly in his chair and grimaces. "My mom was a nurse. She cared so much about her patients. She tried to do right by them, even in a brutal system. It was like I was betraying her, on top of betraying myself.

"I only went the once. When those pills ran out, I tried to gut out the withdrawals. But it was too hard, man. It was too hard to do it alone."

Jake nods. "I know what you mean," he says. "The first time I knew I had a drinking problem—like a real, serious problem—I was eighteen. My band had just blown up the year before, and it had been one long party. I didn't even notice that I was drinking every day, because it's not like I had to go looking for it, you know? Booze was just always there.

"But then we had a little break, and I went home for a few days. And all of a sudden, I was *craving* a drink, every waking moment. Some sleeping moments. Wanting it like I had never wanted anything in my life. It started to feel like maybe I wasn't just drinking on tour because there was alcohol around. That maybe it was something I needed, and needed all the time. It scared the shit out of me. I quit cold turkey. Or that's what I thought, anyway.

"But then the break was over, and the band was back together, and in the studio. The first night we finished recording, someone proposed we go to some bar. I knew perfectly well I should say no. That I couldn't. But I didn't want to admit weakness. I didn't want to be different. So I went. And I got drunk. And I stayed drunk for the next three years."

This time, when Jake looks out into the audience, he finds Charlie's gaze and holds it for a beat. Charlie looks—well, *complicated*, I think. Sad, but like it's a sadness he's used to. That he's spent a lot of time with.

"It's a lot of shame," Jerome says. "Being an addict."

Jake turns to the audience. "That's why having resources is so important. I was lucky—I had people who loved me. And I also had money. When I was finally ready to ask for help, I got sent straight off to Promises, and they were able to help me detox safely. And I got to do multiple stints at rehab because the first time didn't stick for me, like it doesn't stick for most people. But under other circumstances, I might have died waiting for a hospital bed."

That's clearly Jerome's cue, and he starts talking about the resources Elena has put in place to make sure that people in her district who want help are able to get it. Every eye is on him, except mine. I hear the important things he's saying, but I can't stop looking at Jake. He's not running for the door this time. He's not looking to be anywhere other than where he is.

Once Jerome and Jake are done, everyone wants to talk to them. Maya finds me and passes me a plate of what she's deemed to be the best of the passed apps. I'm halfway through it when Charlie joins us and introduces himself. They are, understandably, extremely curious about Jake and me; I try to put them off with polite-but-vague answers for as long as I can. Jake and I don't even know what we are yet.

They're asking me about Gemma, who they've heard a lot about but haven't met, when Jake makes his way over to our huddle. "Sorry," he says. "Being an alcoholic has never made anyone as popular as I appear to be tonight."

"You were amazing," I say. And I can't help myself—I reach out and squeeze his forearm, which flexes underneath my touch. "And so yourself."

"You really were wonderful, Ramsey," Maya says, nodding emphatically. "Thank you for doing this."

"Well, I'm not doing it again anytime soon," he says. "But yeah. I'm glad I did."

Maya seems like she wants to say something else, but her face dissolves into an enormous yawn. "Jesus," she says. "Sorry I'm a little fatigued lately. It's been a long day."

"I was just going to ask if I could get you to go home soon," Charlie says. Then to me, apologetically, "She's been here since like nine a.m."

Jake's gaze flicks over to me. "I was gonna ask Maggie if she wanted to go get dinner anyway," he says. "So we could talk."

I can feel Maya and Charlie's eyes on me, waiting for my reply like they're watching their favorite TV show. "I do want that," I say.

XXII

MAGGIE

We end up at a little diner just a few blocks away, the sort of fifty-year-old spot where we might look out of place in our fancy rich people clothes if we weren't on New York's Upper East Side.

"So," Jake says, once I've ordered a patty melt and he's gotten a Greek omelet. "You came."

"I came." The wild improbability of it—everything that's happened between us—hits me all at once, and a giddy grin spreads across my face. Jake mirrors it, and I reach a hand across the table. He enfolds it in his.

"I couldn't stop thinking about you," I confess. "I know what I said, back at the Cabins, but . . . but I think I was fooling myself. Trying to convince myself that I didn't want more from you. That this was something I could or should just walk away from." Jake's hand squeezes mine. "I don't want this to be something perfect that I had and then gave up," I say. I think of the bouquet I finished this morning: something just as untamed and impossible as whatever's growing at this table between us right now. Even though it won't survive forever, I'm still glad I made it. "I want it to be real for as long as it lasts."

Jake squeezes again before releasing my hand from his. His eyes stay locked on mine. "I want it to last a long time," he says, his voice rough with feeling.

"Me too. As long as you can stand to stay in New York, anyway." I think we're in a place where I can risk teasing him again, and the thought makes every limb go light. I love the idea of having our banter back. Having us back.

Jake laughs. "I know. The Berlin thing—it was a cop-out. But I really have been wanting to stay in one place for a while now. I just needed someone to convince me to stop fucking around and actually do it."

"I've heard I can be very convincing," I say.

"Oh," Jake says. "You can."

Our food interrupts us, and as we eat, I tell Jake about the Halloween-themed wedding I worked on a few weeks ago; he shares about adjusting to full-time city life. His new project is finally, actually learning to cook.

As soon as we're sated, we pay the check in a hurry and spill out onto the street. On the sidewalk, Jake pulls me to him and kisses me like we've been apart for years: long and slow and lingering.

"So," he murmurs against my mouth. "Where to next?" He's acting shy, but there's a gleam in his eye like he knows what I'll say.

"You're really going to make me invite myself over?"

"I was trying to give you options!" he says. "And also, to be honest, my New York place is pretty bare bones. I mean, it's not like Vermont. I'm working on it."

"You know I love a work in progress," I say. "Show me the way."

When we get to the door of Jake's Tribeca loft, I see the flowers in a vase on his doormat and feel the heat creep up my cheeks. A neighbor must have accepted the delivery from my assistant, Viola.

"Those are from me," I say.

"Fuck, Maggie, you do arrangements like *this*? I don't know why I pictured buttoned-up rich people flowers from the way you talked about work and your clients."

My eyes flit between him and the freewheeling exuberant thing I created this morning. "That's what I've been doing," I say. "But I also—I've been trying some new things lately. I got inspired on this trip I took to Vermont. Maybe I'll tell you about it sometime."

He grabs the card and reads aloud, "*I'm proud of you.*"

"I sent them this morning, before I knew if I was coming to the event. And I definitely didn't consider I might be here when you got them."

"Then how did you know you were proud?"

"Because I was proud of you for putting yourself out there and speaking at the fundraiser. For running toward it. That was the point."

He looks at me like it will take him days to process this four-word note and presses his hands to my cheeks. "OK, I should warn you," he says. He bends down to pick up my delivery and unlocks the door. "I bought this place when I was, like, twenty-two," he explains as we take our coats off. "It's supposedly my home base, but I've never been here more than a month at a time . . . so I really haven't done as much with it as I could. As I'd like to."

The space has massive windows with incredible city views and a dining room table laid with long taper candles in modern Lucite holders. It's beautiful, in a soulless way. All the cozy touches of his Vermont A-frame—the stacks of hand-knit blankets, the local ceramics, the detritus of his hobbies—are completely absent.

I notice a dog crate in the corner. "Is that for when Buster comes to visit?" I'm charmed by the thought of it.

"I'm adopting. I put in an application with this shelter in Soho."

I raise a brow. "Small enough to fly under a seat?"

He just smiles. "Like I said, Maggie, I'm staying."

It's my turn to be overcome. "I think now's when you show me your bedroom."

It's a silly line, given that this is an open plan and I can see his king bed in the far side of the space, but Jake takes my hand and leads me over to it anyway.

I spot the deep-red blanket he was knitting on his porch when I came back from my hike. "You finished it."

"And the bookcase too—and that one is a small miracle,

as far as I'm concerned. I told you the blanket was yours if you wanted it, so I brought it here just in case."

I step closer to him and push him to a seat on the mattress. "Remember when we met? When I called myself full throttle?" He smiles, nods. "I hope you're ready for that."

Jake pulls me to his lap, and his hands slide down my body, from my shoulders, along my hips, to my ass, mapping me like I might have changed since the last time he touched me. The space between my legs goes hollow and aching, and I groan into his mouth.

We fall back into bed together, and we can hardly pull apart long enough to wriggle out of our clothes. There's an urgency to having as much skin pressed against each other as possible, but once Jake is sitting up against the headboard and I'm in his lap—both of us naked—with my knees bracketing his hips, it's like time slows down. I wrap a hand around him and start to stroke, firm and slow, pressing a kiss to his neck, then another. I can feel his pulse going against my mouth and against my palm, all of him responding to my touch.

"Maggie," he groans. "God, you feel good."

I run my lips down his cheek and along his jaw, messily smearing kisses across his face until his mouth is pressed into mine. "I love touching you like this," I tell him.

"Don't stop," he says.

"I won't," I promise.

I keep holding him, stroking, my world narrowing to the way his hips get restless, the sweat that's making his hair curl, the sounds he makes when pleasure gets overwhelming. This is the first time he's let me see him like this: face-to-face, my own desire on the back burner for now. He lets me take him apart, piece by piece.

I'm gentle right up until the end, when he's close, when he needs more. Then I reach down and rub my hand through my own wetness, using it to make everything slicker, hotter, faster. "You feel that?" I ask. "That's how much I want you. That's how much I want to feel you."

Jake has been holding my gaze, but as he loses control, his eyes slam shut and he comes over my fingers. He exhales in shuddering pants, and I lean my forehead into his shoulder, catching my own breath.

We're both damp with perspiration, but neither of us pulls apart. Jake slides down into the sheets and draws me with him. I turn on my side and nuzzle my head against his shoulder.

"Thank you for—for being here right now." I think he knows what I mean. Not just physically, but emotionally.

"Maggie," Jake says. "I can tell you with absolute certainty: This is the only place I want to be."

Vacation's not over yet: Read the book's epilogue to find out where Maggie and Jake go from here—plus, the prologue to get a peek into Maya and Charlie's star-studded Brooklyn wedding. Just scan below or visit 831stories.com/vacationself.

More novellas like this one are waiting for you at 831stories.com, where we celebrate romantic fiction in all its forms. You can also dive into bonus content, products, events, and fan fiction and join our membership program to receive new releases early, get discounts across the site, and access all sorts of exclusive perks.

ACKNOWLEDGMENTS

Thank you so, so much to the team at 831: Erica Cerulo, Claire Mazur, Madison Feller, Catherine Krenzer, Angela Vang, Elaine Orihuela, and Marie Joh.

Thank you to Jennifer Prokop and Sanjana Basker for your edits, encouragement, and patience.

Thank you to my friends and family for *your* encouragement and patience. None of it happens without you guys, and none of it means anything without you, either. I love you all very much.

Finally, thank you to everyone whose writing helped me think through Jake's experience with addiction. David Foster Wallace sucks as a person, but his writing about the possibilities of recovery changed my life when I was twenty-two. I also owe a debt of gratitude to The Small Bow and all its contributors. And, of course, to my therapist and Lexapro prescription for keeping me sane enough to write despite my own messy and difficult brain.

ABOUT THE AUTHOR

ALEXANDRA ROMANOFF is a journalist, a cultural critic, and the author of 831 Stories's Big Fan series. She's also written three novels (under Zan Romanoff), most recently *LOOK*, which *O: The Oprah Magazine* called "one of the LGBTQ books that will change the literary landscape." She cohosts the podcast *On the Bleachers*, which examines the intersection of sports and pop culture. Her favorite member of One Direction is Louis Tomlinson. She lives and writes in LA.

If this left you wanting more...

did you know 831 Stories releases a book every month?

Sign up for The Ones:

A membership that gives you early access to every new 831 release—straight to your mailbox, e-reader, or audiobook player. Starting at $10 a month.

The Ones members also enjoy 20% discounts across all of 831stories.com and special access to events, merch, and more.

Join or gift a membership today:

831STORIES.COM/THEONES

ALSO FROM 831 STORIES

Big Fan by Alexandra Romanoff

A high-profile scandal derailed Maya's DC career, and she's eager to fly under the radar—that is, until her former boy-band crush reaches out with a job offer.

Hardly Strangers by A.C. Robinson

One night with a rock star could upend Shera's best-laid plans, revealing how a chance encounter can rewrite a story—and change everything.

Comedic Timing by Upasna Barath

Naina is seeking a fresh start in NYC after breaking up with her girlfriend, but when she meets someone at a party, he's so offtype that her attraction to him fuels an identity crisis.

Set Piece by Lana Schwartz

When a breakout BBC star gets swarmed by fans during a night out, it's a no-nonsense bartender, CJ, who rescues him—and warms them both up for an after-hours hookup.

Square Waves by Alexandra Romanoff

The first spin-off in the *Big Fan* series, an enemies-to-lovers romance in which tabloid fodder mixes with a long-brewing rivalry as Cassidy contends with her high school nemesis.

Exit Lane by Erika Veurink

A postcollege cross-country road trip sparks *something* between Marin and Teddy—though it's not quite clear what. Over the next eight years, they have fated encounters on multiple continents.

Grape Juice by Eliza Dumais

When Alice lands in France for a wine harvest, she's disenchanted with her life. But she soon finds something she's missing in the vineyard owner's nephew Henri, who's just as lost as she is.

Rooting Interest by Cat Disabato

When Felix gets pulled off her NFL beat to cover the WNBA, she doesn't expect to find herself so taken with the sport—or with one of its biggest stars, Natalie Czapski.

Found Time by Caroline Goldstein

Lili and Reid lock eyes after a 1993 Jeff Buckley show. Thirty years and a whole lifetime later, they cross paths once more. Can they finally make their way back to each other?

Major Gift by Tiffany Ezuma

Ndidi, the widow of a billionaire tech mogul, is determined to give her wealth away—and keep one secret from Geoffrey, the perceptive journalist tasked with telling her story.

Down to Earth by Julia Turshen

Vegetable farmer Frankie doesn't know what to make of Paige, the Brooklyn mom who's moved to her quiet upstate town. But could the attraction she's feeling grow into something more?

Double Standard by Mallory Thomas

Ana is about to film a Greek-god epic when a sighting with her co-star threatens her career. Her plan? Fake-date his stunt double, Levi, and let everyone believe *he's* who she was spotted with.

831 STORIES BOOK CREDITS

So many people were involved in bringing this book to life. Many of their names are included here, but there would be no HEA without the passionate work of booksellers and librarians and the enthusiasm of readers. And as we all know, romance readers are the best readers.

831 Stories

Erica Cerulo, Madison Feller, Marie Joh, Catherine Krenzer, Claire Mazur, Elaine Orihuela, Angela Vang

Authors Equity

Andrea Bachofen, Rose Edwards, Carly Gorga, Sarah Christensen Fu, Becca Kadison, Deb Lewis, Madeline McIntosh, Nina von Moltke, Diana Simmons, Erin Vandeveer, Don Weisberg, Craig Young

C47 Design

Phil Chang, Haneu Kang, Jamin Lee, Naomi Otsu, Sunny Park

Editing

Sanjana Basker, Jen Prokop, Lindsey Weber

Marketing, Events, and Publicity

Emma Benshoff, Zoë Gillespie, Tara Larsen, Ashleigh Magee, Kaitlin Phillips, Riley Vaske, Kristin White

Production

Sam Martin, Scribe Inc.

Keep reading for a taste of
Square Waves
by Alexandra Romanoff
from 831 Stories

I

I haven't lived here in a decade, but my parents have kept my childhood bedroom a time capsule: a preserved-in-amber reminder of who I used to be Before. The white lace curtains on the windows are sweet and girly; the vanity mirror has photo booth snapshots of me with high school girlfriends tucked into its frame. There's a literal blue ribbon hanging above the bed, a souvenir of the academic merit award I won as a senior. All the markings of exactly who I was: the kind of girl people love.

I rarely think about that version of me anymore. For the first twenty-two years of my life, Cassidy Weaver wasn't a household name or one synonymous with scandal. But I've been After Cassidy for long enough that that can be hard to recall. Unless, of course, I'm thrust back into rooms where I used to spend most of my time focused on English homework and extracurriculars that looked good on early decision applications.

In so many ways, I know myself better now than I did then. And one thing I'm certain of is that if I don't unpack tonight, I'll spend the next three weeks living out of a suitcase. I force myself from the edge of the bed to the closet, open its door, and groan. How is there still clothing in here? Didn't I take everything with me when I moved to DC for college?

As I scan the relics, I allow myself a moment of tenderness for this former self and her miniskirts so mini, they might as well be belts. Band T-shirts from my short-lived emo phase hang above pairs of *very* aspirationally high heels.

Then I shove it all to the side and start hanging my things—my current things. The Char cashmere sweater I bought with my first big paycheck, the boots I've had resoled three times, and the Issey Miyake dress that will probably always be my best-ever thrift find. I wish I saw the contrast between these two wardrobes as reassuring: a reminder of all of the years that have passed since I lived here. How much I've survived and even grown. But the things I've packed feel like they're from another life too. One I'm not entirely sure I want anymore.

One that might not want me either.

Once I've slid my suitcase under the bed, I give in to the teenage gravity of the room and flop down on my old comforter. When I free my phone from my back pocket, there are no new messages. The last person I heard from was my mom, alerting me that she and my dad were on the plane, headed to Paris for their thirtieth anniversary celebration. *The house is going to be so happy to see you!!* she wrote.

I tap a thumbs-up reply and then unreply and replace it with a heart instead.

Technically, all I have to do this month is unpack my

bags in my parents' Berkeley Craftsman. Starting Friday when I left the office, I officially kicked off the minisabbatical that my boss didn't suggest as much as ordered. It turns out I wasn't the only one to notice my thoughts shifting from *I wonder if I'm burning out* to *I physically cannot make myself function at work.* This break was framed as a gift, but we both know there was an underlying message: *Take a few weeks, get yourself together . . . and if you don't, don't come back.*

My parents aren't aware of the unstated threat. They only know the story that I've been telling them, which is that the time off is a reward for an intense-but-gratifying job well done. I've already consumed my fair share of sympathy and can't risk eliciting more. I have zero desire to see pity on anyone's face ever again if I can help it.

I shift onto my back and fight my first yawn. I'm trapped in that weird in-between time of oncoming jet lag. It's 11 p.m. where I came from but 8 p.m. here. Too early to go to sleep, but my eyelids are getting heavy anyway.

I need to get out of this house if I want to stay awake, but I don't have a lot of options. I've already eaten—my mom left me a square of lasagna in the fridge, which I consumed standing up in the kitchen as soon as I walked through the door.

But . . . a bar, maybe? A drink sounds nice. An adult activity, a reminder that I'm not actually eighteen anymore. And who knows? Maybe I'll meet someone hot. Have a flirtation.

I laugh out loud, alone by myself. Berkeley guys come in three types—nerdy grad student, nerdy techie, and nerdy professor—and none of them are mine. But I roll off the bed, put on my favorite jeans and some mascara, and grab my parents' keys anyway.

There's a mirror hanging above their entryway, and as I head out, I catch a glimpse of myself: my blonde hair in its messy topknot, my cheeks pale because, despite the fact that it's deep summer, I haven't spent an afternoon outside in ages. I look as tired as I feel. But that's fine. I'm not going anywhere fancy. Mostly, getting a cocktail will waste away an hour. And what am I doing here if not killing time?

I haven't lived in Berkeley in a long time and never when I could legally drink, so I have to consult the Infatuation about where to even go. I decide on a comfortingly divey place that, on Sunday night, is busy but not packed. Almost as soon as I slide onto an empty seat at the bar, a bartender comes over to take my order. She has a tragus piercing and a complicated haircut. It's cliché but true: the Bay Area is *so* different from DC. And I have missed it here.

"Do you know what you want?" she asks.

I bite my lip, like this is a trick question. In college, I drank vodka sodas; AC (After Cooper) I learned that that was a sorority girl tell and switched to gin and tonics. But my go-to doesn't feel like the right thing for this moment. It suddenly seems so . . . East Coast blasé. But then what *do* I want? A beer? A glass of wine? Is this a celebratory drink or a mournful one, and how do I even—

My ruminating is interrupted by a hand on my shoulder. A man's voice near my ear, low and pleased with itself. "Do you need help ordering, Cassidy?"

I whirl around and find myself face-to-face—uncomfortably close, nose-tip-to-nose-tip, he-can-probably-smell-my-breath close—with Leon Park.

The first thing my traitor brain thinks is, *Handsome.* Which, to be fair, is an accurate reaction to Leon's presence. He was hot in high school, and he's even hotter now. His thick black hair has grown out into perfectly tousled waves. His eyes are still amber and still sparkling. He smirks at me, and it's equal parts disarming and infuriating. I'm both grateful and annoyed that I tried even a little bit before coming here tonight.

Thank god he drops his hand and steps back, creating some distance between us so that I have room for a second thought: *Oh, Jesus Christ, no.*

It wouldn't be fair to say that Leon and I were nemeses back in the day because that would indicate that he cared about me. But we did annoy the shit out of each other, our opposite personalities creating friction every time we so much as spoke. I would have avoided him if I could, but my teenage best friend Willa dated his best friend Zeke for *all four years of Berkeley High* . . . only to break up a few weeks after graduation, when it was too late to do me any good.

It's been almost a decade since I've been in Leon's proximity, but his presence kicks me into gear, and I hear the words "I'll have a martini" coming out of my mouth before I have a chance to consider the thought.

A martini? Where the hell did that *come from?*

The bartender reaches for a glass. "Vodka or gin?" she asks.

"Gin." At least this part I know. "Botanist, if you have it."

"Sure. How dry do you want it?"

"Oh. Um. Medium dry?"

"Olives?"

My neck goes hot. What is this, the Spanish Inquisition? "Sure."

She looks over at Leon. "And you?"

"I'll have a PBR, please."

I know he's just ordering a beer, but it still feels like he's trying to show me up by getting something simple and unfussy that doesn't require a litany of follow-up questions. Leon is the chillest bro ever to chill. And I am *not*. That's one thing that Before Cassidy and After Cassidy have in common: an inability to live up to every California girl's birthright and just, like, go with the flow, man.

Leon turns so that his back is against the bar. He props himself up on his elbows and stretches his long legs out in front of him. His jeans are so worn, they're almost—but not quite—ripping at the knees, and his Vans are authentically skate-scuffed. His eyelashes are soot black against his cheeks as he blinks at me.

"What are you doing here?" he asks.

I look for accusation in his tone, but he actually sounds curious. I'm still not letting my guard down. "Having a drink."

"Oh, so we're being *literal* tonight."

"What else would we be?"

"Excuse me for making conversation."

I can't help it: I roll my eyes. "Since when do you want to talk to me in the first place?"

"Cass. Please." Only people who know me from Before call me Cass. I correct everyone else, to ward off any creep toward unearned intimacy.

Leon smiles like he means it, and a pinprick of a dimple forms on his right cheek. There's a corresponding uptick in my heart rate. God*damnit*. I hate this guy for a lot of reasons, and the way my body responds to his has always been one of them.

He slips a hand into his front pocket. "Anyway, I could ask you the same question."

Before I can consider his response, the bartender is back with our drinks. My glass looks unwieldy, a clear, shallow pond of gin sitting atop a long, thin stem, and I wish again that I'd ordered something else. Maybe Leon will leave me to go meet up with friends? Or some sun-bleached Instagram model with a surfboard strapped to her truck and a side gig reading tarot cards?

But my luck has always been shitty, and he hops up onto the barstool next to mine.

"Well, to answer the question you didn't ask, I live here," he says. "Same as I always have."

"So is this your local?" Because of course I would walk into his regular haunt.

"Nah. I was supposed to meet up with Zeke, actually, but he bailed last minute. I was already halfway here, so I figured may as well." He gestures at the baseball game on the TV, and I watch the shape of his shoulder moving under his T-shirt. Leon was skinny in high school, all limbs. He's still got some of that teenage lankiness about him, even though we're nearing thirty.

"So you and Zeke are still close."

"Yeah. We try, anyway. He had a kid last year, and it's—he's a really good dad. But his wife works nights, so it's just . . . getting time with him is hard."

"Holy shit. Zeke's a dad." The idea makes me a little dizzy. If Zeke is already that kind of adult . . . I try not to play the comparison game, but I am toeing the starting line.

"Does he still have—" I gesture at my hair. In high school, Zeke's trademark was a gelled mohawk, always dyed the loudest possible colors: sunset pink or fluorescent orange.

"Nah. Kept it for the wedding just to prove a point, but it's too much maintenance. It's buzzed down super tight right now. You might not recognize him anymore. He just looks like a regular guy."

I'm too stunned to say more than "God, I guess we are grown-ups."

"Sure are, Ms. Martini." Leon's tone is a little too pointed. There goes that nice nostalgic moment we were having.

"It's just a cocktail."

"And you haven't touched it."

I haven't. The glass is precariously full; I have no idea how the bartender got it over here without spilling. Under other circumstances, I would just slurp some directly off the surface, but not in front of Leon. I refuse to let him see me as anything less than adept.

So instead, I pick it up delicately and raise it to my mouth in slow motion, my lips pursed. I know I must look ridiculous. It takes what feels like a full minute for me to manage a sip.

When I do, it tastes cold and floral and salinated. Perfect. I put the glass back down and close my eyes for a second.

When I open them, I expect Leon to mock me for something—my pincer grip on the stem, maybe—but he's just . . . looking at me. His gaze is glued to my mouth. I know it's not possible, but I'd swear his irises are a few shades darker.

"Good?" he asks.

"Yeah."

Leon looks away and takes a long pull on his beer. "So you still haven't told me what you're doing here. Are you not going to answer simple questions tonight?"

"I don't think I am." As childish as it is, I can't help but enjoy getting a rise out of him. There was a time when the only thing that could shake Leon from his lazy surfer posture was getting irritated with me. That kind of power is hard to resist.

"Will you answer complicated questions, then?"

"What's a complicated question? Like, you want my thoughts on Bay Area housing? For me to weigh in on the political issues of the day?" I wince as soon as I say it.

I very specifically *don't* want to talk politics with Leon or anyone. It's way too easy to jump from someone's opinion of President Knight's second term to the scandal that almost kept him from getting elected in the first place.

Wasn't that when Cooper Abbot fucked his wife's college intern?

Wasn't that intern . . . me?

I'm anticipating a sharp retort. But Leon sighs and shakes his head. "You know, it's actually been kind of a long day," he says. "So if I were going to ask you a complicated question, Cassidy, it might be: Why does it seem like you hate me so much? Still?"

I'm startled. Obviously Leon knows I don't like him. It's not hard to miss. But the way he says it—I don't know. It almost sounds like he *cares*.

"I don't hate you" is all I can muster, even if it isn't true. "And once again, I could ask you—"

"You could," he says. "But I asked you first."

He shifts toward me slightly, and I catch a whiff of his scent: Old Spice and skin. I'm hit between the eyes with a memory from over a decade ago: a summer evening at the beach, a bonfire burning. Leon and a bunch of boys stripping off their shirts and sprinting into the ocean screaming. How they ran back, drenched, and launched themselves at us, the knot of girls gossiping on a blanket. Leon landed half on top of me, and the water streaming off him was freezing, but he was warm. He smelled exactly the same then, and I still remember the twist I felt in my stomach. The rush between my legs.

He's giving me a perfect opening to say something smart, or mean, or both. And I'm tempted to take it. To pick up my less perilously full glass and just walk away.

But the truth is, for the last six years, everyone in the world has had an opinion about me. Some people think I'm an evil slut who destroyed an innocent man's career with her wiles; some people think I'm a victim of the patriarchy who needs to be saved. But they're all working off a media narrative—articles they read or podcasts they listened to. I've contributed to some of that with my work with the nonprofit Kindness Is Better, or KIB, sometimes penning my own op-eds and doing public speaking. I've made being Cassidy Weaver, "Gen Z's Monica Lewinsky," my entire career and a good chunk of my actual life.

But Leon actually knows me. Knew me, at least. Whatever he doesn't like about me is hard-earned.

An unwelcome thought: *If only you didn't despise him so much, he really would be the perfect hookup.*

I mentally bat it away and take another sip of my drink before responding. If I was less tired, I might be able to come up with something clever. But I only have it in me to tell the truth. "Okay, well. You didn't like me. So I didn't like you back."

Leon raises an eyebrow. "When did I give you that impression?"

As if he's completely innocent here. "Oh, I don't know, when you made fun of my seventh-grade history presentation grade for being *too detailed.*" Instantly, my cheeks go hot. I can't believe he goaded me into admitting that I'm still hung up on some barb from half a lifetime ago. But it was the first semester of middle school, when impressions mattered deeply. Plus, I might have already developed a tiny crush on Leon. To have him notice me but only to make fun of me—well. Clearly it left a mark.

For some reason, he doesn't seize the opportunity to tease me. "Why did you care what I thought?" His elbow moves closer to mine. "I almost failed that class."

I narrow my eyes. I knew Leon wasn't a hardworking student, but he always gave off the aura of being so smart that he didn't have to study. I assumed he got effortless A's and that if he didn't, it was because he was too cool to care about something as lame as grades.

"People like boys who fail way better than girls who succeed," I say with a shrug. At the time, it felt like he was putting a target on my back, pointing out to everyone, *This one tries too hard.* And of course, because I am who I am, I only doubled down after that. And I went even harder when Leon was around.

"That's true."

I'm so surprised to hear him agreeing with me—about anything, even something as obvious as the basic dynamics of sexism—that I drink half my martini in a single gulp. "Be careful," I quip, sliding the olive from its skewer. "Next thing you know you'll be apologizing to me."

"Do you want me to?"

I squint at Leon, and I feel like I actually see him for the first time all night. He's sun-browned, his skin darker than it ever was in high school, in a way that makes me wonder if he works outside. When he smiles, crow's-feet crinkle at the corners of his eyes. He's wearing a long-sleeved shirt, and it's shoved up on one muscular forearm; I see the edge of a tattoo there, a suggestion of all the ways he might have changed in the last ten years that aren't visible to me yet.

If we were strangers, just meeting, I would be following the thing I feel between us: this gentle, insistent desire to get closer. I would be angling my body toward his. Maybe our legs would brush or I would touch his thigh.

The next steps are well trod. Immediately after Cooper, I was depressed, and then for a while, I was reckless. I slept with anyone I wanted to and some people I kind of didn't. I know exactly how to map the route from a barstool to a bedroom.

But Leon and I are not strangers. Hardly. Which makes this even more precarious . . . and, in some ways, even more enticing.

I lean an elbow on the bar, put my chin in my hand. My drink is mostly gone, and I feel loose. Relaxed for the first time in months.

"What would a Leon Park apology even look like?"

He smiles at me, huge, dimple on full display. "It would look like me saying, 'I'm sorry, Cassidy.'" He reaches out and pats my knee. My breath catches in my throat, and I think he notices because he leaves his palm there just a half second too long. Like maybe he's gauging my reaction.

Like maybe he wants to keep touching me.

"I appreciate that."

"Honey, you want another one?" the bartender cuts in.

My gaze is locked on Leon, and if I was feeling like myself, I would say no. I would think, *Go home, Cassidy*, and then do it.

But between burnout and jet lag, gin and desire, the last six years and the last twelve hours, I'm not entirely sure who *myself* is. So instead, I say, "Yes, please."